The Diviners

A Play in Two Acts and Elegies

by Jim Leonard, Jr.

SAMUEL FRENCH

FOUNDED 1830

New York   Hollywood   London   Toronto

SAMUELFRENCH.COM

THE DIVINERS
was written with the support of
the Indiana Arts Commission

THE DIVINERS was first developed and performed by the Hanover College Theatre Group under the direction of Tom Evans and with the support of the American College Theatre Festival. The set was designed by Tom Evans. Tracy Dedrickson designed the lighting. Costumes were designed by Katy Matson, and Robert Padgett designed the sound.

BUDDY LAYMAN .... *John Geter*
JENNIE MAE LAYMAN .... *Dee Meyers*
FERRIS LAYMAN .... *Keith White*
C.C. SHOWERS........................ *Doug Rogers*
NORMA HENSHAW .... *Susan Leis*
DARLENE HENSHAW .... *Valerie Sherwood*
BASIL BENNETT .... *Mark Fearnow*
LUELLA BENNETT .... *Shannon Robinson*
GOLDIE SHORT .... *Liz Hans*
MELVIN WILDER .... *Mark Bock*
DEWEY MAPLES........................ *Clint Allen*

THE DIVINERS was first professionally produced by the Circle Repertory Company in 1980 under the direction of Tom Evans. The set was designed by John Lee Beatty. Jennifer von Mayrhauser designed the costumes. Areden Fingerhut created the lighting. James M. Arnemann was the stage manager.

BUDDY LAYMAN .... *Robert MacNaughton*
JENNIE MAE LAYMAN .... *Lisa Pelikan*
FERRIS LAYMAN .... *Jimmie Ray Weeks*
C.C. Showers .... *Timothy Shelton*
NORMA HENSHAW................ *Jacqueline Brookes*
DARLENE HENSHAW .... *Laura Hughes*
BASIL BENNETT .... *Jack Davidson*
LUELLA BENNETT .... *Elizabeth Sturges*
GOLDIE SHORT .... *Mollie Collison*
MELVIN WILDER .... *Ben Siegler*
DEWEY MAPLES .... *John Dossett*

CHARACTERS

BUDDY LAYMAN — an idiot-boy

JENNIE MAE LAYMAN — his sister

FERRIS LAYMAN — their father, a mechanic

C.C. SHOWERS — a backsliding preacher

NORMA HENSHAW — owner of the Hoosier Dry-Goods, a
true believer

DARLENE HENSHAW — her neice

GOLDIE SHORT — owner of the Dine-Away-Cafe

BASIL BENNETT — a farmer, the local doctor of sorts

LUELLA BENNETT — his wife, a doubter

MELVIN WILDER — a farmhand

DEWEY MAPLES — a young farmhand

SETTING

The play takes place in the homes, fields, and public gathering places of the mythical southern Indiana town of Zion, population forty. A small and rural community with a few houses and farms along the river.

The entire play takes place on one set without any carry on tables or chairs, etc. The set should be raked and smooth enough for an actor to pull himself over it on his belly. The starting point for the design should be the final scene.

LIGHTING

Lights should convey time, place and mood. A sky would be nice.

All the night scenes, and there are several, happen during full moon. So the night light can be fairly bright and still believable.

The river light must be an absolutely solid swash of color with a definite depth line. The well light, which attunes us to the use of light as water, should probably be a lighter shade of river-color.

PROPS

The Cafe can be dealt with by simply giving the proprietor a tray with several coffee cups, etc. All the Dry-Goods needs is a jar of jelly beans and a small sack of healing salts. There's no need for line on the fishing poles.

Anything live, such as the birds, worms, etc., should simply be assumed and seen in the eye of the actor.

STYLE

These are good and simple people. They have nothing but the best of intentions.

6

The Diviners

FIRST ELEGY

(*A dulcimer plays "Amazing Grace" as the lights rise. There are two pin spots: one isolating* BASIL *and the other on* DEWEY. *The farmer and farmhand speak directly to the audience but not to each other; they speak as if they know the people in the theatre the way a man knows his neighbors. The dulcimer fades into the story:*)

BASIL. Now. Just before Buddy Layman passed beyond us there was a storm to the sky like no other. I was workin out to the back fields, down along the crick there, when I first felt the air start to changin. I looked at the clouds. I heard the wind blowin. And I says to myself, "Basil," I says, "Don't stand out here like a fool to the field. Get the tools to the barn fore the storm hits!"

DEWEY. And I run like the wind right after the boy died. Callin all over town for his father. I fly by the Dry-Goods and on through the Diner, lookin clean over Zion to find him.

BASIL. So I set the tools down and I turned my head to see the air all in motion above me. I'm standin there, near the barn there for shelter, and the clouds're as dark as the land is long — circlin and swirlin like a fire to the sky!

7

DEWEY. And I looked!

BASIL. And I seen it!

DEWEY. And I hollered!

BASIL. And I knew!

DEWEY. I says, "Ferris! Ferris! He's dead now for certain." (*A moment. Then quietly:*) Buddy Layman . . . he's passed on beyond us.

BASIL. (*Softly.*) And like a slate wiped clean or a fever washed away where there was fire to the sky now there's nothin . Where there was clouds there's just blue and the sun.

DEWEY. His only son gone and it's me who brings the word when Ferris comes to his door in the mornin . I seen him there like he's a wood stick carvin in the wood frame door and they're welded together in grievin . I says, "Ferris . . . I'm sorry." And he don't move and don't speak. I says, "Yor son, he's passed on beyond us." (DEWEY's *light fades. He exits. Moonlit night as* BASIL *speaks:*)

BASIL. The idiot boy is dead, don't you see? Buddy Layman's gone. There's no tellin the weather. When he said it would rain we layed our fields in rows and we knew it would be a good season. You see, a man works, a man waits, and he hopes and he plans, but it was the boy who told us the weather. And that boy . . . he was somethin . Somethin else for a fact. He couldn't talk for two cents or take the time to tie his shoes, but he seemed to know things you figured nobody knew. Without drillin rigs or men with machines — without nothin but a willow rod in his hands — Buddy Layman came onto my land in late spring and he set himself to witchin a well. Call it vein-findin , water-witchin , smellin , seekin or divinin , . . . the boy had a touch and a feel for water.

ACT ONE: THE EARTH AND THE WATER

(*The boy searches for water with a long forked
stick. He overlaps and repeats the word "water"
three times whenever it is mentioned during the
dowsing. His head is turned up and his eyes are
nearly closed as he follows the sense of the stick.*
DEWEY, MELVIN, *and* LUELLA *enter and are immediately involved in the scene:*)

BUDDY. Water water water . . .

BASIL. Come on, boy. You'll find her.

DEWEY. (*To* MELVIN.) Would you look at him go?

MELVIN. Witchin ain't nothin. It's that stick there
that does all the work, Dew.

DEWEY. Like hell it's the stick.

MELVIN. Like hell if it ain't.

DEWEY. Bud knows what he's doin.

MELVIN. He knows next to nothin.

DEWEY. Hell if he don't.

MELVIN. Hell if he does.

BASIL. If you fellas keep up this ruckus you'll throw
the boy off! Now how many times have I told you
tonight this dowsin's a delicate business.

LUELLA. I doubt he's gonna find any water.

BASIL. Luella, the signs're all right on the money. It's
a full moon, it's May, not to mention a wind from the
east.

LUELLA. The signs don't find water. You want water
you hire a drill rig.

BASIL. Luella.

LUELLA. We've been chasin around through the fields
half the night and there's no sign of nothin at all.

BASIL. Just give the boy time.

LUELLA. How's he gonna find any water whin he won't even touch it? He don't wash, he don't bathe. The boy's dirt head to toe. I mean, Basil, he's not even baptized.

BASIL. That's cause he feels it right to the bone, don't you see?

BUDDY. (*Sudden.*) Water. He feels water!

DEWEY. He's on it now, Basil!

MELVIN. He's on it but good!

BUDDY. He's on it!

DEWEY. You'll find her!

BUDDY. He'll find her!

MELVIN. Let the stick show you!

BASIL. Come on, boy!

DEWEY. Water!

BUDDY. Find water!

MELVIN. Water, boy!

BUDDY. Water!

LUELLA. Lord, Basil!

BUDDY. Water!

BASIL. You'll find her!

(*The* WELL-DIGGERS *coach the boy on, building on the suggested lines for them below, as the stick reaches higher and higher.* BUDDY'S *entire frame tenses as he comes closer and closer:*)

BUDDY. Water! Find Water! Ground, you got to give water! Water, ground! Water! He's got to find water! Now, ground! Give water! Water! Water, ground! Now!

WELL-DIGGERS. Come on, Bud! You'll find her! Dowse it, boy! Water!

(*The stick suddenly begins to bend. Everyone falls silent. The stick bends nearly in half:*)

LUELLA. (*Softly.*) Sweet Jesus in Heaven would you look at that?

(BUDDY *drops the stick and drops to his knees, exhausted:*)

BUDDY. He got you some water . . . he got you some.
BASIL. You done just fine, boy. You done fine by me.
BUDDY. He's a good guy, Basil?
BASIL. You're a good guy, Buddy Layman.
BUDDY. Wooboy!
MELVIN. (*Shaking the boy's hand.*) You hit her right on the money!
DEWEY. (*Shaking the other hand.*) You done real good, Bud.
MELVIN. Done a damn fine job. Damn fine.
BASIL. (*Partial overlap.*) Let's get to work —
DEWEY. I never saw such a job.
MELVIN. It's a hell of a job.
BASIL. (*Taking charge.*) I'm not payin you boys to stand around cussin and shakin hands half the night. Now run up the barn and get the shovels.

(MELVIN *and* DEWEY *run off.* BUDDY *starts to follow:*)

BUDDY. You want him to help you?
BASIL. (*Stopping the boy.*) You done your fair share, Bud. Now you can tell your Dad I'll be sendin over a dozen or so bushels a corn and wax beans come this fall. You remember to tell him I thank you.
BUDDY. You thank him?
BASIL. I thank you, my friend. (BASIL *exits to the barn.* LUELLA *has the stick:*)

LUELLA. Hey, honey? You wouldn't want a show Luella how to work thes thing would you?

BUDDY. How to work it?

LUELLA. How to make her find water.

BUDDY. (*Demonstrates.*) Well . . . he shuts his eyes.

LUELLA. (*Holds the stick out and does so.*) Yeah?

BUDDY. And he thinks on his Mama.

JENNIE MAE. (*Calling from off-stage, as if the boy's in the distance.*) Buddy—?

LUELLA. Your Mama?

JENNIE MAE. Buddy—?

LUELLA. You think a her whin you try to find water?

(BUDDY *crosses to his sister as she enters. The two scenes, one at the well and one at the Layman's happen on opposite sides to the stage. The sun's beginning to rise:*)

JENNIE MAE. I can't take my eyes off you for two seconds, little brother, without you're runnin off all over the fields.

BUDDY. Well, he's playin , Jennie Mae.

JENNIE MAE. (*Holds the broom out.*) And you're supposed to be sweepin .

BUDDY. What're we gonna do with that boy? He can't do nothin right, Jennie Mae. See that broom right there? He couldn't make it get to workin . And you seen how he done with his shoes.

JENNIE MAE. Buddy.

BUDDY. (*Pulling his shoes out from under the set.*) His sister says, "Buddy, you keep them shoes on your dogs. Them feet ain't supposed to get naked." And would you look how he does like he's dumber than dirt?

(MELVIN *and* DEWEY *enter with a post hole digger and a shovel. There should be a trap where the boy*

divined water. As the farmworkers dig they step in-
to it, working their way deeper and deeper:)

JENNIE MAE. Don't call yourself names.

BUDDY. He can't help it he's daffy.

JENNIE MAE. Now Bud.

BUDDY. He's a looney litte coot for sure.

DEWEY. Let's get to workin.

JENNIE MAE. Let's get your boots on.

BUDDY. He don't want to wear boots.

JENNIE MAE. Buddy.

MELVIN. Let's get some dirt into it, Dewey.

DEWEY. (*Referring to a shovelful.*) It's a good chunk
a diggin.

MELVIN. There ain't enough dirt there to hide a worm,
Dewey.

DEWEY. Listen, Melvin. I'm at thes hole workin . I'm
standin here sweatin and you're doin nothin but lean
on that post holer.

MELVIN. You tryin' to say I don't know how to dig,
huh? You tryin' to tell me what's what with a shovel?
Will listen, Dewey, I been through the best damn
trainin Uncle Sam's got to offer. Got sent through basic
trainin two times in a row. Now I may not know much
nut I know what's what with a shovel.

DEWEY. Then why don't you use it?

MELVIN. Why don't you give me a little room, Dew?
Give me a little room, pal, I'll tear this hole up.

(BASIL *enters with another shovel. He takes charge*
immediately:)

BASIL. Would you fellas shut up and get diggin for
water?

LUELLA. You're not gonna find us a well out her,
Basil. There's nothin but mud in that hole.

BASIL. Luella.

LUELLA. I tried this stick, Basil. I give her a shake and it's worth next to nothin . You're wastin your time on that hole.

JENNIE MAE. Take your time with those laces.

BUDDY. Well he can't make 'em tie.

LUELLA. Buddy Layman's not crazy. He's just smart enough to fool with you, Basil. Leave you diggin out here after nothin . When a farm needs a well you got to use a machine.

(DEWEY *is in the trap. They pass him tools as if in delicate surgery:*)

DEWEY. Shovel.

MELVIN. Shovel.

LUELLA. Even a fool knows that folks need a drill-rig for water. Sticks and shovels get you nowhere in this land.

DEWEY. Post holer.

MELVIN. Post holer.

LUELLA. Indiana is nothin but rocks and mud, Basil. Clean down to China it's rocks and mud and mud and rocks and it takes a full sized drill rig to dig down to water.

BASIL. Put your back at it, Dew.

LUELLA. But no, you wouldn d listen. You won't use a machine. And there you all sit to your elbows in mud and plain to see you're gettin nowhere but dirty.

BASIL. Lean into it, Dew. Heave some weight on it, boy—

DEWEY. (*Partial overlap.*) Basil, hold it! Hold on . . .
(DEWEY *lowers himself completely into the well as* SHOWERS *enters on the other side of the stage. He carries two beat up old suitcases. He's worn out:*)

BASIL. Water . . .?
SHOWERS. (*Looking at the sky.*) Lord God A'mighty.

(*A light shines up from the well:*)

DEWEY. (*Amazed.*) My feet're gettin wet . . . !
BASIL. Water! Luella, there's water!
LUELLA. Water.
BUDDY. He did it! He tied em! (BUDDY *jumps up and there is simultaneous celebration at the well and at the Layman's.* SHOWERS *remains where he is:*)

BASIL. Water. I told you he'd find it.	BUDDY. Tied his shoes by his self!
MELVIN. Waaaooo!	JENNIE MAE. You're a good boy.
BASIL. We hit the vein!	BUDDY. He tied em!
DEWEY. Water!	JENNIE MAE. You sure did!
MELVIN AND DEWEY. Waaaaoooooo!	BUDDY. He's a good guy!

BASIL. Grab the shovels, boys! Let's get a drunk on!

(*The* WELL-DIGGERS *exit and* BUDDY *grabs the broom. He sweeps enthusiastically as* SHOWERS *crosses to the Layman's:*)

SHOWERS. Lord God in Heaven I'm tired.
BUDDY. Tied his shoes by his self, he's gonna sweep by his self! He's sweepin and sweepin —
JENNIE MAE. Buddy, stay on the porch.
BUDDY. He's cleanin his yard, Jennie Mae.
JENNIE MAE. Buddy.

BUDDY. He's sweepin and sweepin . . . (BUDDY *sweeps into* SHOWERS.)

SHOWERS. Hi.

BUDDY. Hi . . .

JENNIE MAE. Can I help you with somethin ?

SHOWERS. Well, to tell you the truth, Ma'am, I'm lost.

JENNIE MAE. What you lookin for?

SHOWERS. I'm not lookin for nothin too special here, Ma'am. I'm just kinda curious where I am at the moment. (SHOWERS *is a bit of a fast-talker:*) I had me a fitful night a dreamin , you see, got myself all turned around in my sleep. And when I woke up this mornin I looked at the road one way there and then I turned and took a look up the other — and what do you think I said?

BUDDY. What?

SHOWERS. I says, well, I'm fit to be tied if Indiana don't look all the same no matter which way you turn! I says to myself, "C.C. Showers," I says, "You're about as lost on this road as a small ball in tall grass. Just stuck up like a boot in the mud." Couldn't tell comin from goin or which end was up — till I seen my friend over here givin the grass the once over. And I says, "Now there's a man who cares about the land that he stands on." I says, "Here's a fella who can tell me where I am."

BUDDY. (*Proud.*) You're at Buddy Layman's house.

SHOWERS. I had a sneakin suspicion I might be.

BUDDY. Yeah. It's his house alright. Them's his windows, his door, his porch. And this girl right here? She's his sister.

JENNIE MAE. Buddy.

BUDDY. You gonna sweet talk her, Mr? You want him to maybe get lost?

JENNIE MAE. You just get back to sweepin .

BUDDY. Aw, he's tired a sweepin .

SHOWERS. You know you can't be too clean, pal.

BUDDY. Huh?

SHOWERS. I says a fine and upstandin young fella like yourself ought to love keepin clean.

BUDDY. You ain't gonna wash him?

JENNIE MAE. Are you sellin soap or somethin. Mister?

SHOWERS. No, Ma'am.

BUDDY. You ain't gonna put him in water?

SHOWERS. In water?

BUDDY. Jennie Mae, don't let that guy wash him!

JENNIE MAE. Now what do you want a go scarin him for? He never done nothin to you!

SHOWERS. Now wait a minute—

JENNIE MAE. You just come walkin up here out of a clear blue and go teasin folks you don't hardly know!

SHOWERS. Now hold the boat, Ma'am! I only stopped cause I'm lookin to help folks!

JENNIE MAE. Are you one a them Mormons?

SHOWERS. To put it real plain, Ma'am—I'm in need of a job.

JENNIE MAE. Well, we're not givin handouts.

SHOWERS. I'm not wantin a handout, I'm wantin to work! You name it, I'll do it. Yard work, house work, cleanin or mowin. I'll milk the chickens, I'll pluck the cows. (*Pause.*) I'm willin to work the whole day for just food. I'm not a big eater. Little tiny portions. To look at me eat you'd think I was raised by the birds. A crumb here, a crumb there.

BUDDY. (*Concerned.*) Ain't you had you some breakfast?

SHOWERS. Not lately, my friend . . .

JENNIE MAE. Maybe you better talk to my Daddy.

SHOWERS. If it wouldn't put you to no trouble.

JENNIE MAE. (*Exiting.*) S'no trouble at'all, Mister.

BUDDY. What's your name, Mister?

JENNIE MAE. (*Calling, on her way off-stage.*) Daddy?

SHOWERS. C.C.

BUDDY. You think you're maybe gonna stick around awhile, C.C.?

SHOWERS. It all depends, Bud.

BUDDY. They's lots a stuff here you know?

SHOWERS. There is, huh?

BUDDY. Yeah! They's lots a good stuff. You see the woods over ther don't you?

SHOWERS. Bud, I sure do.

BUDDY. Well that's where the birds live.

SHOWERS. Do they, now?

BUDDY. Yeah! Way up the trees they do. Way up the leafs.

SHOWERS. Now that's a good thing to know.

BUDDY. You see the ground right there don't you?

SHOWERS. Mr. Layman, I do.

BUDDY. Well that's where the doddle bugs are.

SHOWERS. Well, you're just chock-full a knowledge, my friend.

BUDDY. He thunk he might be.

SHOWERS. (*As if he didn't hear right.*) I beg your pardon?

BUDDY. He says he thunk he might be.

SHOWERS. (*Unsure.*) Now you're talkin about you?

BUDDY. Yeah. Can't you hear him?

SHOWERS. Yeah. Yeah, pal, I hear you.

BUDDY. You see the sky up there, pal?

SHOWERS. Bud, I'm lookin right at it.

BUDDY. You know who lives up there?

SHOWERS. Who?

BUDDY. (*Amazed.*) Jesus.

SHOWERS. Way up there?

BUDDY. Jesus Son a God does.

SHOWERS. What do you figure he does up there, Bud?

BUDDY. (*Thinks this over.*) Well . . . he's maybe got him a little house.

SHOWERS. (*Interested.*) Yeah?

BUDDY. Yeah. Maybe got him a runnin toilet inside.

SHOWERS. Now that's a good thing to have.

BUDDY. He thunk it might be.

SHOWERS. Mr. Layman, it does my heart good to meet a man who knows his way around the Church.

BUDDY. We ain't got no Church, C.C. Don't you know nothin ?

SHOWERS. Your Mama taught you the Gospel at home, huh?

BUDDY. His Mama?

SHOWERS. Yeah.

BUDDY. (*Concerned.*) You ain't seen her?

SHOWERS. No . . .

BUDDY. He can't find her nowhere, C.C.

SHOWERS. (*Gentle concern.*) How long she's been gone?

BUDDY. Well he ain't sure no more. He looks in his house and his yard and the woods and he can't find her nowhere.

SHOWERS. Well, I'd imagine she'll be home before long, don't you think?

BUDDY. Sometimes he hears her. Sometimes at night he hears her right there . . . and her voice is right there . . . like he can touch her almost, when he's sleepin . . .

SHOWERS. (*Gentle.*) You mean your Mama's passed away, Bud?

BUDDY. You know where she is?

SHOWERS. Well . . . I'd imagine she's livin in Heaven.

You know what angels are, don't you?

BUDDY. What?

SHOWERS. Angels're what we call the people in Heaven. The folks on beyond us, you see?

BUDDY. What's angels do?

SHOWERS. For the most part they all tend to fly around singin .

BASIL. (*Likes this idea.*) Angels can fly?

SHOWERS. That's what they say.

BUDDY. Like the birds?

SHOWERS. Like the birds.

(FERRIS *enters. He's a greasy mechanic.* BUDDY *runs to him:*)

BUDDY. Hey, Dad, she's up to the sky! His Mama's flyin with Jesus!

(FERRIS *might swing his son around some. He enjoys playing with the boy. Likes teasing him:*)

FERRIS. You're gonna be up to the sky like to never come down, you don't finish your chores before noon, boy.

BUDDY. Well he's talkin to C.C.

FERRIS. You made you a friend, huh?

BUDDY. (*A secret.*) That guy ain't had nothin to eat, Dad.

FERRIS. (*Eyes him over.*) So you're the fella that's lookin to work, huh?

SHOWERS. (*Crosses to* FERRIS, *hand out to shake.*) C.C. Showers, sir.

FERRIS. Ferris Layman, Mr. Showers. Chew tobacco?

SHOWERS. No, sir.

FERRIS. (*Taking a plug out.*) Well, you oughta! A man wants to work in a garage then he's gotta chew somethin . Can't hire a fella that's prissy.

SHOWERS. (*Takes the plug.*) Thank you kindly.

FERRIS. It's a good tastin' plug, huh?

SHOWERS. (*It tastes awful.*) Real tasty.

FERRIS. Don't swaller it, Mister! Hell, the whole point's to spit!

SHOWERS. Beg your pardon.

FERRIS. Too late, huh? Can I get you some water?

SHOWERS. I'm fine. Just fine.

FERRIS. I'd offer you more but with Hoover in office there ain't a lot more to be had, huh?

SHOWERS. I hear you.

FERRIS. (*Making sure.*) You're a democrat, ain't you? Not votin for Hoover?

SHOWERS. Not by a long shot.

FERRIS. I don't mean to be nosy but no man votin' for Hoover is workin for me.

SHOWERS. Folks vote for Hoover there'll be nobody workin .

FERRIS. Damn Hoover. Those government guys don't know shit from shine-ola.

SHOWERS. Nope.

FERRIS. Here we sit with half the damn country wound up as tight as a shock spring and Hoover won't let a man drink.

(BUDDY *has found his way to the two suitcases. He is sitting between them:*)

BUDDY. Ain't you figure they's maybe somethin to drink in these boxes?

SHOWERS. Well, they're mainly full a nothin , my friend.

BUDDY. Ain't you figure they's maybe a little rootbeer down in em?

FERRIS. Don't be so darn nosy.

BUDDY. He ain't gonna hurt nothin , Dad. He's gonna haul em around some. Like he's a helper, you know? Like C.C.

SHOWERS. Make a deal, my friend?

BUDDY. Word a Honor, C.C.?

SHOWERS. You can haul these cases around town for awhile if you promise to bring 'em right back.

BUDDY. (*Serious.*) Lick your hand, C.C. (BUDDY *licks his palm and holds it out.* SHOWERS *understands, does the same, and they rub palms together in a solemn vow of sorts.* BUDDY *then walks and talks his way off- stage with the cases:*) Ain't gonna drop these boxes for nothin . No sir. Ain't gonna nose down inside em or bang em up nohow. He knows they ain't no rootbeer down in em. He's a good guy, that Buddy. Word a honor, he is.

SHOWERS. (*Smiles.*) I'd imagine bein a Daddy gets to be a full time business.

FERRIS. Hell, there ain't nothin to it. I raise em like weeds.

SHOWERS. Like weeds, Mr. Layman?

FERRIS. You can pull em or trim em or hedge em on back some, but you're best off to just leave em go. You ever seen a weed that ain't healthy?

SHOWERS. No.

FERRIS. Same way with kids. If a car breaks, you fix it — if a tire's flat, patch it. But kids're just fine on their own.

SHOWERS. Mr. Layman, I take it you like cars.

FERRIS. Mr. Showers, I love em. Nash, Buicks, DeSotos — you name it. Plus there's a whole world a tractors. Your John Deere, Farm-All, Fords a course.

SHOWERS. Yeah—
FERRIS. Nothin like a good solid engine.
SHOWERS. No sir.
FERRIS. You ever tear down a six banger?
SHOWERS. That's quite an engine.
FERRIS. Hell of an engine. Course a flathead'll put it to shame.
SHOWERS. I'd imagine.
FERRIS. Can you rebuild a flathead?
SHOWERS. Is that a car or a tractor? (*Pause.*)
FERRIS. Never heard of a flatheaded tractor.
SHOWERS. It's a car, huh?
FERRIS. (*Suspicious.*) Can you at least tear down a carburator?

(SHOWERS *shakes his head.*)

FERRIS. Fuel pump? Ignition?
SHOWERS. Well—
FERRIS. Steerin or tires?

(SHOWERS *shakes his head.*)

FERRIS. You can't patch a damn tire? Where the hell a you been?
SHOWERS. I been walkin, Mr. Layman, for close to three months. I hardly rode in a car, let alone try to fix one. But I'm needin a job awful bad, see? Just enough work to feed me.
FERRIS. If I knew what you did it might be I could help you.
SHOWERS. Well there wasn't much work back in Hazard, Kentucky. I mean, I quit what I did, see?
FERRIS. Quit a good job for nothin?
SHOWERS. I couldn't do it no more.

FERRIS. You walked off the job when there's no work for miles?

SHOWERS. I had to leave.

FERRIS. (*Pushing.*) Did they fire you?

SHOWERS. No —

FERRIS. Did you run in the law?

SHOWERS. I just couldn't keep workin.

FERRIS. What the hell'd you do?

SHOWERS. (*Nearly angry.*) It don't matter no more!

FERRIS. (*Starts to walk away.*) I can't hire a man don't know what he does.

SHOWERS. I'm lookin to start all again, don't you see? I been lookin to work the whole time I been walkin .

FERRIS. You're wastin my time, mister. (*Starts to exit.*)

SHOWERS. Listen, Mr. Layman. To tell you the truth . . . I's a preacher.

FERRIS. Teacher?

SHOWERS. No. A Bible-totin preacher. (*Pause.* FERRIS *smiles:*)

FERRIS. Aw now, you're full a shit.

SHOWERS. I ain't preachin no more though—

FERRIS. You full a shit, ain't you?

SHOWERS. I quit! I give it up altogether! (FERRIS *smiles.*) I ain't preached for three months in a row, Mr. Layman. Went close to twelve years then I quit, now I'm done.

FERRIS. You really a preacher?

(JENNIE MAE *enters with her brother in tow. The boy has both suitcases, but they're significantly lighter:*)

SHOWERS. I was! I ain't preachin no more, though.

BUDDY. (*Protesting.*) Word a honor, Jennie Mae! Word a honor!

FERRIS. A Bible bangin, Jesus jumpin, Heaven and hellfire preacher!

JENNIE MAE. You tell Mr. Showers the truth Buddy Layman!

BUDDY. He ain't done nothin wrong!

JENNIE MAE. (*Gives her brother a whack on the tail.*) Just you tell him.

BUDDY. (*Demonstrating.*) Well . . . He was just walkin , see, C. . . . C? Till his arms get to feelin kinda lousy, see. So he says, maybe he'll feel better, he gets him some rootbeer. On account a them boxes're heavy and his arm's hurtin somethin awful . . .

FERRIS. You didn't take somethin outta those cases now, boy?

BASIL. (*Innocent.*) No siree, Dad. They ain't nothin in em.

FERRIS. Nothin in em?

BUDDY. Nope. Not no rootbeer nor nothin . (*He sets the luggage by* SHOWERS *and holds up his hand in the sign of the pledge.*) Word a honor, C.C.

(SHOWERS *opens the suitcases. They are empty.*)

FERRIS. You mean the boy dumped all you stuff out?

SHOWERS. They're a little easier to carry now, yeah.

FERRIS. All your clothes?

JENNIE MAE. Your blankets—

SHOWERS. My bedroll—

BUDDY. Your Bible—

SHOWERS. My Bible.

FERRIS. Everything?

SHOWERS. Seems to be the case. (*Slight pause.*)

BUDDY. (*Innocently.*) Well . . . he figures he better take him a little walk for now, Dad.

FERRIS. (*Grabs the boy's arm.*) Hold still a minute, Bud.

BUDDY. He don't want a sit still!

FERRIS. Well you're gonna sit still till you tell us what you did with his things, boy.

SHOWERS. Now Mr. Layman.

FERRIS. Now some things don't irk me, Mr. Showers, but stealin the clothes off the back of a preacher ain't quite on my list a sittin still for.

JENNIE MAE. A preacher!

FERRIS. A marryin-buryin, readin-revivin, devil and damnation preacher, Jennier Mae. And your little brother, who somebody was supposed to be watchin, just stole everything the man owns!

JENNIE MAE. I can't be watchin him all the time, Daddy.

FERRIS. I can't be watchin him either.

JENNIE MAE. I dress him, I feed him, I walk him all over the place—

BUDDY. He don't want a sit still!

JENNIE MAE. I need time to spend with my friends, damnit!

FERRIS. Would you knock off the cussin? He's a preacher I told you.

JENNIE MAE. I don't care if he preaches!

BUDDY. Stop screamin!

JENNIE MAE. I'm not screamin!

FERRIS. This man's a preacher!

SHOWERS. Now hold it! Hold the boat, will you? (*All commotion stops. He preaches:*) I was a preacher, but I ain't preachin now. I don't do prayers or lead songs and I give up on sermons. It's no sin to change and I've changed! (*Slight pause.*) I give it up. (SHOWERS *picks up his luggage and starts to exit:*)

BUDDY. Ain't you gonna stick around here some?

SHOWERS. I come this far. I'll get by just fine.

JENNIE MAE. With no clothes?

FERRIS. Without nothin?

BUDDY. Aw, C.C., don't leave him.

SHOWERS. (*Stops.*) Aw now, Bud.

JENNIE MAE. He could sleep in the barn, Daddy.

SHOWERS. No, I don't mean to burden.

FERRIS. I don't mean to take offense, but my barn ought to be good enough for a good man to sleep in.

JENNIE MAE. (*Exiting.*) I'll get you some blankets.

SHOWERS. (*Crossing back to* FERRIS *and the boy.*) Now listen, Mr. Layman. I'm willin to work for my keep, see?

FERRIS. And I'm willin to make you keep workin, C.C. (FERRIS *takes one of the suitcases and exits to the barn.* BUDDY *starts to follow:*)

BUDDY. Come on, C.C.

SHOWERS. Hey, Bud. You don't happen to have any idea where you might a walked with my things do you?

BUDDY. Nope. How bout you?

SHOWERS. You sure you don't know?

BUDDY. He knows where theys birds at though C.C. Out the barn—way up the roofters. Theys big birds and little birds, baby birds and mamma birds—theys flyin all over like angels.

SHOWERS. (*Exiting with the boy.*) No, now the angels're way up in Heaven there, Bud, and the birds're here in Indiana.

(NORMA *enters singing "Rock of Ages". She mops the floor in her store as she sings.* LUELLA *enters and watches* NORMA *mop.* NORMA *should stop singing abruptly as* LUELLA *finishes her speech;*)

SHOWERS. (*Continued.*) It's a whole world a difference, my friend.

NORMA.
"Rock of Ages, cleft for me,
Let me hide myself in Thee;
Let the water and the blood,
From Thy wounded side which flowed
Be of sin the double cure,
Cleanse me from it's guilt and power—"

LUELLA. (*Overlapping.*) I know why you're singin, Norma Henshaw. You're singin and cleanin the whole Dry-Goods top to bottom on account a that new slick-talkin preacher.

NORMA. Luella.

LUELLA. Now, Norma, for all we know this guy is a smooth-talkin con man. We don't know nothin about him.

NORMA. We know he's a preacher.

LUELLA. What Church is he with?

NORMA. Why Luella, he's a Christian a course.

LUELLA. Well that doesn't mean you can trust him you know.

NORMA. I been prayin for this for ten years in a row. I don't ask the Lord much, I don't pester him, see? But I have made a few small requests. The Lord knows how the town needs a preacher, Luella.

LUELLA. But what kind a preacher'd work in a garage?

NORMA. Well we can't afford to be picky.

LUELLA. Be picky!

NORMA. We been ten solid years without singin or savin or baptizin, period. The lord's answered our prayers, don't you see?

LUELLA. Well I don't know, Norma.

NORMA. Don't be so darn doubtful, Luella. So down in the mouth. Why, just look at Goldie next door. She's been spickin and spannin for days in a row just to let that man know how he's welcome.

(SHOWERS, BUDDY, *and* FERRIS *enter:*)

GOLDIE. Why you fellas're just as welcome as welcome can be.

BUDDY. Got any rootbeer here, Goldie?

GOLDIE. What kind a Diner'd I run without rootbeer?

BUDDY. Pretty lousy.

GOLDIE. (*Handing him one.*) Well it wouldn't be the Dine-Away-Cafe. Just made some fresh coffee, boys.

FERRIS. Coffee sounds fine.

GOLDIE. I'd expect you been showin our new friend around town, huh?

FERRIS. Ain't much to see.

GOLDIE. Why there's the Dry-Goods and the Diner and the view a the river. Not to mention the place where the Church was. You seen the Church ain't you?

SHOWERS. Guess it must a slipped by me.

FERRIS. Ain't nothin left but the foundation, Goldie.

GOLDIE. (*To* SHOWERS.) Well before she burned down, it was somethin I tell you. That Church had a steeple so high it put the tree tops to shame. And people? There was people all over. Those bells got to ringin and the whole town was full. Did a real good business on Sunday.

SHOWERS. You don't say?

GOLDIE. Fed more people on Sunday than the whole week together. Those Church folks're real big eaters. You want some pie with that coffee.

SHOWERS. No thanks, Ma'am. I'm fine.

GOLDIE. Apple pie, peach pie, rhubarb and cherry—whatever you wants on the house.

FERRIS. Well I'd like a donut.

GOLDIE. Plain donut's a penny, Ferris. Glazed're two cents.

FERRIS. Plain, thank you.

BUDDY. How bout you get him a rootbeer?

GOLDIE. (*A little surprised.*) You're not done with that last one?

BUDDY. Ain't no more down in it.

GOLDIE. You're gonna throw off your whole constitution, you know that? You drink and drink and drink and drink—you will make yourself irregular. (*She hands him a rootbeer.*)

BUDDY. You regular, Dad?

FERRIS. Hell I'm fine.

GOLDIE. (*Crossing off to get a donut.*) No cussin.

SHOWERS. That Goldie's quite a woman.

FERRIS. Well she's pretty but she's pushy.

SHOWERS. I noticed.

FERRIS. Ain't nothin worse'n a damn woman gets pushy.

GOLDIE. (*Entering with a donut.*) You're gonna cuss you can eat this outside, Ferris.

FERRIS. It's a awful good lookin donut.

GOLDIE. Don't you dare bite that donut.

FERRIS. I'm gonna pay you.

GOLDIE. You know the rules just as well as I do "No drinkin—"

FERRIS AND GOLDIE. "No Cussin" and "You Pray Before You Eat—"

FERRIS. (*To* SHOWERS.) Keeps em posted right there on the sign.

GOLDIE. Care to pray?

SHOWERS. I beg pardon?

GOLDIE. It's only right for the guest to say grace over meals.

SHOWERS. Well, Ma'am, this ain't exactly a meal.

GOLDIE. Well you're still the guest.

FERRIS. Just give her the grace, huh?

SHOWERS. You give her the grace.

FERRIS. I'm no good at prayin.

SHOWERS. It's your donut, Ferris.

GOLDIE. It's my Diner. I'd like for our guest to say grace.

SHOWERS. Ma'am, you don't understand—

GOLDIE. You don't pray, he don't eat. (*Slight pause.*)

FERRIS. Listen C.C. I'm really kind a hungry.

SHOWERS. I know.

FERRIS. Well just run off a quick one.

SHOWERS. Aw, Ferris—

FERRIS. It's just a donut, C.C.—won't take you but a second.

GOLDIE. Bow your heads. Shut your eyes, Buddy. Pastor Showers? (*All heads are bowed but for Showers. Buddy's eyes are closed, no real semblance of prayer. SHOWERS looks straight ahead, eyes open. After a moment he says quite simply.*)

SHOWERS. Thanks for the donut.

FERRIS. Amen. (*Slight pause. Suspiciously:*)

GOLDIE. What Church're you with?

FERRIS. Goldie, the man means to give up on preachin.

GOLDIE. Give it up?

SHOWERS. Yes, Ma'am.

GOLDIE. You mean to quit?

SHOWERS. I mean to stop altogether! (*Slight pause.*)

GOLDIE. In that case the coffee'll cost you a nickel.

SHOWERS. It's a good cup coffee.

FERRIS. I got her.

SHOWERS. (*To* BUDDY.) You bout ready to go, pal?

(BUDDY *has taken one of his shoes off:*)

BUDDY. He ain't goin nowheres till his dogs feel better.

SHOWERS. What's a matter?

BUDDY. He's itchin.

SHOWERS. (*Looking at the boy's foot.*) Looks like a touch a the ivy.

BUDDY. Itchin like crazy, C.C.!

GOLDIE. All the boy needs is a tub a hot water. I been sayin that much for years.

BUDDY. Huh?

GOLDIE. Fever weed, salts, and a hot tub a water.

BUDDY. (*Lying.*) He ain't itchin no more.

GOLDIE. You'll be itchin all over, you don't soak those feet.

FERRIS. Hell, I'm dirt head to toe and I'm fine.

GOLDIE. It ain't right not to wash.

FERRIS. Does he smell? Does he stink?

GOLDIE. That ain't the point, Ferris.

FERRIS. Half the world's made a dirt and it ain't hurtin nothin. The damn roads're all dirt, the fields're dirt. Even Hoover's got a mud pie for brains.

GOLDIE. Don't make fun a Mr. Hoover in my Diner, Ferris. Badmouthin the president's the same thing as cussin. Same exact thing to a T.

SHOWERS. Kind a fond of him, are you?

GOLDIE. I couldn't care less if Herb Hoover got hit by a truck in his sleep. But he's still the president and I won't have him badmouthed.

FERRIS. Now what'd I say that's so awful, Goldie?

GOLDIE. I'm not about to repeat it.

BUDDY. Said hell, said damn, said Hoover—

GOLDIE. You see there! You see what it leads to?

FERRIS. Bud can cuss if he wants.

GOLDIE. He's just a boy, Ferris.

FERRIS. When I was his age I cussed all the time.

GOLDIE. He's only 14.

FERRIS. And I'll tell you what else, I'm a better man for it.

GOLDIE. You are the most bull headed man in the world, Ferris Layman.

FERRIS. A man can't cuss, he can't hardly talk.

GOLDIE. What would your wife say? (*Pause. With true concern:*) The way you raise the boy, Ferris . . . it ain't right for him.

FERRIS. (*Softly.*) Well Sara ain't here no more, Goldie.

BUDDY. (*Softly.*) Dad?

FERRIS. What you need, son?

BUDDY. Dad? S'gonna rain.

FERRIS. (*Gentle.*) Change a the weather'd be nice, Bud.

BUDDY. They's clouds up there, Dad. S'gonna rain somethin awful.

SHOWERS. Bud, the sky's awful blue.

FERRIS. (*Softly.*) It'll rain.

BUDDY. Can't you feel the clouds? It's gonna storm somethin awful.

GOLDIE. Lord knows we could use it.

(DEWEY *and* BASIL *enter with hoes as the others exit:*)

SHOWERS. Not a cloud in the sky.

DEWEY. Rain, Basil.

BASIL. Rain, huh?

BUDDY. Can't you feel the clouds?

DEWEY. It's what the boy says.

BUDDY. (*Exiting.*) Gonna rain.

BASIL. How'd he look when he said it?

DEWEY. Well. He was scratchin his feet somethin awful.

BASIL. Seemed pretty sure did he?

DEWEY. I come walkin up the garage, I says, "How you doin, Bud?" He says, "It's gonna rain."

BASIL. Well . . . the alfalfa's in at least.

DEWEY. Yeah.

BASIL. But the rutabaga's not near.

DEWEY. It ain't even close.

BASIL. Figure you boys can get that highland turned?

DEWEY. S'awful rocky.

BASIL. I know.

DEWEY. Full a rocks.

BASIL. Get her turned before the rain comes, give you eighty cents a day.

DEWEY. Damn.

BASIL. A little rain'll be nice, huh?

DEWEY. I guess.

BASIL. Yeah.

DEWEY. Hey, Basil. Look at the sky, will you?

BASIL. Pretty.

DEWEY. There's no clouds for miles.

BASIL. It'll rain soon enough, Dew. The boy knows.

DEWEY. How you figure that is?

What's that?

DEWEY. I mean, you done your fair share a doctorin, Basil.

BASIL. I'm no doctor, son. Most things'll heal alone.

DEWEY. But how do you figure the boy knows like he does?

BASIL. He just feels, I guess.

DEWEY. Feels the weather?

BASIL. Close as I can figure it, yeah.

DEWEY. It's that drownin, you figure? I mean, a fella falls in the water so young like he did—

BASIL. Don't take long underwater to change you.

DEWEY. I guess.

BASIL. He was under awhile, you know. The boy was only three, maybe four, and he was under that water some time.

DEWEY. Jesus.

BASIL. It was his mother that kept him from drownin, you know . . . she died in the water. It's a strange kind a thing.

DEWEY. It's kind a scary almost. I mean, Basil, the way the boy is now—

BASIL. Listen, Dewey, you can't think like that, son. Sometimes things happen—there's no way to stop em or change em, nothin better for tryin. If a boy knows the weather you got to call it a blessin. It's a blessin.

DEWEY. Yeah. Yeah . . . the place'll look awful nice, a little rain on the fields.

BASIL. We get that highland seeded she will.

(JENNIE MAE, SHOWERS, *and* BUDDY *enter.*)

DEWEY. It's good land on the rise there.

BASIL. Yeah, the farm's lookin fine.

SHOWERS. There's nothin so fine as the woods in the summer.

BUDDY. You see all the birds?

JENNIE MAE. Yeah, I see em.

BUDDY. You see that one there?

SHOWERS. That's a blue bird, my friend.

BUDDY. How come he's flyin?

SHOWERS. We scared him, I guess.

BUDDY. Hey, bird. Where you goin? Don't hide in them trees.

SHOWERS. Whoa now—

(BUDDY *follows his bird off-stage:*)

BUDDY. Hey, you bird! Come on back here! Why you flyin from Buddy?

SHOWERS. Hey, Bud—

JENNIE MAE. Oh, Buddy's alright.

SHOWERS. Bud—?

JENNIE MAE. Buddy gets in the woods he's not about to sit still.

SHOWERS. Well . . . this old back a mine ain't about to go chase him.

JENNIE MAE. Oh, you're not that old, Mr. Showers.

SHOWERS. I been feelin it lately.

JENNIE MAE. Well, come here. I'll rub your back some.

SHOWERS. (*A little embarrassed.*) Oh . . .

JENNIE MAE. Now stop moanin and groanin and sit yourself down. Come on. It'll do you some good to sit still. (SHOWERS *sits. She rubs his shoulders:*) There you go. How's that now? A little better maybe?

SHOWERS. Oh . . . I'm dead and in Heaven.

JENNIE MAE. You just been workin too hard.

SHOWERS. Naw—

JENNIE MAE. Yeah, you have.

SHOWERS. Oh—

JENNIE MAE. You're like to work all the time, Mr. Showers.

SHOWERS. (*Softly, dismissing the idea.*) Shit.

JENNIE MAE. What?

SHOWERS. Little work never hurt nothin.

JENNIE MAE. I never heard you talk like you been today.

SHOWERS. Use those kind a words all the time when I'm thinkin.

JENNIE MAE. You think in swear words?

SHOWERS. I think worse things'n that.

JENNIE MAE. Is that why you give up on preachin?

SHOWERS. That ain't quite how I'd put it.

JENNIE MAE. Don't you believe in the Bible?

SHOWERS. I was raised on the Bible, Miss Layman. My Daddy's a preacher and his Daddy before and his Grandad and right down the line. Boy comes to be seventeen or eighteen there's no questions asked — hand him a Bible, turn him loose on the world. He'll make his way fine. Be an awful fine preacher. (*Slight pause. To himself:*) Be just like his Daddy I guess . . . (*He begins to preach as the memory builds:*) My Daddy . . . now he was a preacher. He had folks up on their feet and out a their seats and singin and stompin and life was just fine. Man took to a Bible like he was there just to shout it. Gonna tell everybody! Everybody bout the wonder and the miracle and the sweet love a Jesus! He'd say now you there, Miss Layman, don't you love that sweet Jesus? Don't you love him so much you could cry? Well sure you do! I said sure you do! I said come on up front here and tell us about it! Tell the whole Church how you love that sweet story! Bring em all up front! Let em all tell the story! No sin's a great sin cause all men are sinners! Yes, Ma'am! That's all men! I said all men! I said every last man is a sinner! (*He catches himself. Slight pause:*) Then there's me . . . I'm up front the Church and I'd shout somethin out and they'd "Amen!" right to me. I'd shout and they'd shout and then all a sudden . . . it's dead quiet. I mean they're lookin and waitin and all ready to holler. And there's me up there . . . thinkin! Plain forgot I was preachin.

JENNIE MAE. No—

SHOWERS. Yeah! Plum forgot where I was. Sometimes two or three minutes at once. I tell you, Miss Layman, I think too much.

JENNIE MAE. Think too much?

SHOWERS. I am all the time thinkin! And thinkin and preachin don't mix too well, Ma'am.

JENNIE MAE. Well I never read too much Bible, but you surely can fire it up, Mr. Showers.

SHOWERS. I'm thirty years old, I never done nothin else! All I'm good for is talkin, Miss Layman. Runnin on at the mouth, just jawin away . . .

JENNIE MAE. I think you talk real nice.

SHOWERS. The whole time I was preachin you know what I felt? Nothin.

JENNIE MAE. Mr. Showers—

SHOWERS. I felt nothin, you see?

JENNIE MAE. You still sound awful nice.

SHOWERS. Aw, I need to learn to shut up. (*Pause. Then quietly:*) Well, damn it.

JENNIE MAE. What's a matter?

SHOWERS. I just can't shut up! I guess you're just too nice to talk to.

JENNIE MAE. Now don't tease me.

SHOWERS. Miss Layman—

JENNIE MAE. You make me feel like an old maid when you call me "Miss Layman."

SHOWERS. Well you're awful formal yourself, ain't you?

JENNIE MAE. I'm younger'n you. I'm suppose to.

SHOWERS. Here we are in this day and age—with tractors and light bulbs and Singer Sewin Machines—and you're talkin like any man older'n you's automatic a Mister right off the bat!

JENNIE MAE. Now don't be rilin me up, Mr. Showers. Girls sixteen years old can't call men by first name. Least not in Indiana they don't.

SHOWERS. Then let's just pretend it's Kentucky.

JENNIE MAE. Mr. Showers, I can't!

SHOWERS. We'll say that old beech tree down the way's the door to a mine shaft, and that gulley right there's an old coal train.

JENNIE MAE. Oh, Mr. Showers.

SHOWERS. Come on now.

JENNIE MAE. I can't.

SHOWERS. Sure you can.

JENNIE MAE. No I can't.

SHOWERS. Well, I don't see why not. (*Pause. She looks in his eyes:*)

JENNIE MAE. You want me to?

SHOWERS. I want you to call me by name. (*Light sound of thunder:*) Did you just feel somethin?

JENNIE MAE. Yeah. Yeah, I felt somethin . . .

SHOWERS. Was that a rain drop you figure?

JENNIE MAE. What's that?

SHOWERS. Would you look at those clouds, Jennie Mae? Right up through the break in the trees there.

JENNIE MAE. Oh, my Lord.

SHOWERS. We best find your brother fore the sky splits wide open.

JENNIE MAE. He's on his way home.

SHOWERS. (*Calling Loudly.*) Buddy—?

JENNIE MAE. He's not gonna stay in the woods if it's stormin.

SHOWERS. Buddy—?

JENNIE MAE. C.C., come on! If he's home alone he'll be scared half to death!

(*They run off-stage as the thunder builds and the lights change. The thunder grows louder and louder. BUDDY enters calling frantically for his family:*)

BUDDY. It's rainin! Hey, Dad, it's rainin! Ain't they nobody here? Ain't they nobody hear him? Dad? Jennie Mae? It's rainin outside! He can't breathe right no more. It's rainin! (*He wraps himself up in a blanket and lies down, struggling for breath. He should be completely covered by the blanket:*) It's rainin it's rainin it's rainin . .

(SHOWERS *and* JENNIE MAE *run on as if coming in from the storm:*)

SHOWERS. Woooeee! Never saw such a storm! Like to split the sky open!

JENNIE MAE. Buddy?

FERRIS. (*Entering on the other side of the stage.*) I tell you, it's wild out there!

JENNIE MAE. Buddy?

FERRIS. (*To* SHOWERS.) Wind's blowin like crazy.

JENNIE MAE. (*Sees him and goes to him.*) Buddy, look at you. You must be scared half to death. It's alright. We're here now.

(FERRIS *crosses to the boy, concerned.*)

FERRIS. Hey, Bud.
JENNIE MAE. You're fine now. We're here.
BUDDY. Mama . . . ?
JENNIE MAE. You're alright.
BUDDY. Mama . . . ?
JENNIE MAE. It's Jennie Mae.
SHOWERS. (*Crossing to them.*) Is he alright?
BUDDY. It's rainin.
FERRIS. You're fine, son.
BUDDY. It's rainin.

(*The three of them are grouped around the boy.
BASIL and LUELLA enter on the other side of the
stage. As if watching the storm from their porch:*)

LUELLA. Lord knows how we need this.
BASIL. It's an awful fine rain.
FERRIS. Go to sleep, son.

(NORMA *and* DARLENE *enter. As if watching the rain
from their window:*)

NORMA. (*Reading from a Bible.*) "And the Spirit of
God moved on the face of the waters."
DARLENE. And the Spirit of God was there in the
waters.
BASIL. You see there? The way the ground soaks in
the water.
FERRIS. Just relax now.
JENNIE MAE. Go to sleep.
NORMA. "And God said, Let the waters under the
Heavens be gathered together."

DARLENE. And God said let the waters be together.

BASIL. The highland's all turned and the seeds're all in.

LUELLA. It's bound to be a good season.

SHOWERS. He's asleep now?

JENNIE MAE. He's asleep.

BASIL. Yeah, the farm's lookin fine.

LUELLA. Be a real good summer.

NORMA. "And God saw it was good."

DARLENE. And God saw it was good. Aunt Norma?

NORMA. Darlene?

DARLENE. I thought we already did that one.

NORMA. That was for light.

DARLENE. God thought all of this stuff was pretty good, huh?

NORMA. In the beginning, yeah.

(BUDDY *wakes up as the women exit. He's alone on stage, middle of the night, and realizes he's itching:*)

BUDDY. Hey . . . he ain't sleepin . . . ain't sleepin no more, he's itchin, hey, hey he's itchin all over. Dad? He ain't sleepin! His foots are itchin awful! Jennie Mae? C.C.? Get up!

(JENNIE MAE *and* SHOWERS *enter from opposite sides of the stage. She might be in a night shirt.* SHOWERS *might carry his shoes and have his shirt unbuttoned:*)

JENNIE MAE. Hey now, Buddy.

BUDDY. He's itchin like crazy!

SHOWERS. Calm down, now.

JENNIE MAE. Hush now. You're gonna wake Daddy.

BUDDY. He's itchin!

FERRIS. What the hell's all this belly aching, boy?

BUDDY. Can't you hear him? He's itchin his head off!

FERRIS. And you're makin more noise then a half-blowed out Buick. Now settle down, will you?

BUDDY. Can't you make him all better?

FERRIS. Bud, you'll be fine if you just get some shut eye.

BUDDY. He ain't lyin down, Dad.

FERRIS. You're gonna do like I tell you.

BUDDY. He ain't tired a bit!

FERRIS. Now don't back-talk me, boy.

BUDDY. He ain't gonna sleep. You can't make him.

FERRIS. I'm gonna give you to ten, Bud. You hear me?

BUDDY. Aw, Dad.

FERRIS. I says, One. Two.

(JENNIE MAE *takes* BUDDY *back to his quilt and tries to talk him into lying down. The boy hits the hay just short of the ten count:*)

FERRIS. Three. Four. Five, Six. Seven. Eight's awful close. Nine! Nine and a quarter. Nine and a half! Nine and three quarters!

J.M. Come on, Little brother

BUDDY. Aw, he's itchin just awful.

J.M. Just lie yourself down.

BUDDY. He ain't tired a bit!

J.M. He's almost to ten, Bud!

BUDDY. He's sleepin, he's sleepin!

(*Slight pause.*)

SHOWERS. You drive a hard bargain, Ferris.

FERRIS. Aw, I don't know, C.C. You gotta be headstrong when you're dealin with Bud.

(JENNIE MAE *stays with her brother. The men cross away.*)

FERRIS. (*Continued.*) You never had you no kids.

SHOWERS. Naw.

FERRIS. Never had you a wife.

SHOWERS. Ferris, I'm all I can handle.

FERRIS. Don't you like women much?

SHOWERS. All the women I courted were in church, Ferris. You can't sweet-talk em one night and preach at em next.

FERRIS. Well there's plenty a time, huh? Used to be I didn't know nothin either. I mean, when I went to marry I didn't know a damn thing. I can tell you that now cause I'm older, you see, but at the time I thought I was a genius. Women or horses or cars or what have you. I's the first one to tell you what's what. You know how I asked her to marry? How I married the wife? I says "I love you. I want you. Let's go." I didn't know the first thing about women, C.C.

SHOWERS. Were you sure that you loved her?

FERRIS. Was I sure that I loved her?

SHOWERS. I mean, bein so young . . .

FERRIS. I was crazy about her. Ain't a day that goes by I don't think a that woman. Lie to bed in the mornin, I think how she was. See the house, see the kids, you can't help but remember. I was head over heals in love . . . (*Pause.*) Never came cross my mind I could lose her, I guess. You wake up one mornin and she ain't there no more . . . but you still keep on lovin, you see? I mean, she made me so happy. She's my darlin, my Sara. And nothin on earth gonna change it. (*Pause.*) Course now bein a husband was a piece a damn cake compared to bein a Daddy full time. I wasn't married a year and she give me a daughter. I was just gettin used to a wife.

BUDDY. Hey, Dad?

FERRIS. Then the boy came along.

JENNIE MAE. He's not gonna sleep, Dad.

BUDDY. Dad, he's still itchin. His footbones, his anklers, he's itchin all over.

SHOWERS. You know it could be those salts're the thing the boy needs.

FERRIS. We go soakin his feet, he'll be screamin for days.

SHOWERS. We can't leave the kid go.

FERRIS. Look, I know he needs washin, but there's no way in hell you're gonna get him near water.

SHOWERS. Well it's worth a try ain't it?

FERRIS. You can try all day long but you're not gonna change him!

BUDDY. Hey, Dad! He's still itchin!

FERRIS. This hollerin here's like a whisper, you see?

BUDDY. He's itchin just awful.

FERRIS. Would you quiet down, Bud?

BUDDY. Well it hurts him. (BUDDY *quiets down.* FERRIS *kneels beside the boy.*)

FERRIS. (*Softly:*) Lay back down now and try to get some shuteye. We'll talk in the mornin. Alright? (FERRIS *tussles the boy's hair. He exits.*)

JENNIE MAE. Goodnight, now.

SHOWERS. Goodnight.

BUDDY. (*Itching.*) You guys ain't gonna sleep!

SHOWERS. Aw, Bud. What say we have us a walk and a talk, pal? Keep your mind off your dogs a while.

BUDDY. Where you want a walk at, C.C.? (BUDDY *climbs on Showers's back.* JENNIE MAE *folds the blanket.*)

SHOWERS. Just outside a while.

JENNIE MAE. You two be careful out there in the dark now.

SHOWERS. Goodnight.

(DARLENE *enters. A bit flirty:*)

DARLENE. Evenin, Pastor Showers.

SHOWERS. Evenin, Darlene.

DARLENE. I can't sleep for nothin when the moon's shinin down.

SHOWERS. (*Exiting with the boy.*) It's warm weather for sleep.

DARLENE. (*Watching him go.*) Don't I know it?

JENNIE MAE. (*Crossing to* DARLENE.) Did you sneak out a the house?

DARLENE. (*Innocent.*) I'm just lookin for trouble.

JENNIE MAE. At this time a night?

DARLENE. It's the best time I know to find trouble. I seen the preacher man standin out here on the porch. He couldn't be no better lookin, Jennie Mae.

JENNIE MAE. Oh, Darlene.

DARLENE. I'd be up all night long if that guy lived at my house. Be walkin in the stars so bad I'd bump into walls. I tell you, for a preacher he sure is good lookin.

JENNIE MAE. His eyes sure are somethin. It's like they change colors sometimes when he sees you.

DARLENE. (*Impressed.*) Jesus. There's just somethin about an older type man.

JENNIE MAE. (*Worldly.*) Yeah, he's pretty mature.

DARLENE. Not like these boys around here.

JENNIE MAE. Who you courtin, Darlene?

DARLENE. Just these boys around here.

JENNIE MAE. Not Melvin Wilder?

DARLENE. (*Coy.*) I might be.

JENNIE MAE. Dewey Maples?

DARLENE. I could be. Why don't you come see?

JENNIE MAE. I'm awful tired, Darlene.

DARLENE. Well you don't have to be so darn prissy about it.

JENNIE MAE. (*Exiting back into the house.*) I been up half the night.

(MELVIN *and* DEWEY *enter.* DARLENE *turns and imitates her friend's words to them in Scarlet O'Hara style:*)

DARLENE. "I been up half the night." She just got eyes for the preacher.

DEWEY. Jennie Mae likes the preacher?

DARLENE. Listen, Dewey, she doesn't just like him — she likes him. But don't tell her I told you, okay?

MELVIN. What, do you think Dewey here can't keep a secret, Darlene? You think Dewey's gonna go blabbin all over?

DEWEY. I won't tell her, Darlene.

MELVIN. (*Hands him a flask.*) Have a drink, Dew.

DEWEY. Alright.

DARLENE. Ain't you guys never heard a the Dry-Laws?

MELVIN. Darlene, you're talkin to a veteran a the Army a the U.S. of A. and I'm tellin you the Dry-Laws mean next to nothin. I mean a drink's just a drink, huh? Give her the hootch, Dew.

DARLENE. I'm not touchin that hootch.

MELVIN. (*Challenging.*) What're you scared of a drink?

DARLENE. (*Takes the bottle.*) I ain't scared a nothin.

(MELVIN *pulls* DEWEY *aside as she drinks.*)

MELVIN. Now, you see how that is, Dew? Girls're tricky business. Real tricky business. But you gotta let em know how you stand, see? Now you want a take this girl dancin. You want to take Darlene to the dance.

DEWEY. I'm not sayin I love her or nothin.

MELVIN. But you gotta let her know what you're thinkin.

DARLENE. Hey, Melvin?

MELVIN. We're tryin to talk man to man. You understand?

DARLENE. What're you talkin about Melvin?

MELVIN. We're talkin on how nice you're lookin, Darlene. My pal Dewey, he can't hardly stand it. Now you see how that is, Dew?

DARLENE. You really think I look nice, Dewey?

MELVIN. Tell her how it is, pal. Tell her you mean business.

(DEWEY *crosses to* DARLENE, *very shy:*)

DEWEY. Hey, Darlene.

DARLENE. Hey, Dewey.

DEWEY. I don't love you or nothin.

MELVIN. Dewey, what're you sayin?! That's not what he's meaning, Darlene.

DARLENE. (*A little upset.*) Well what are you meanin?

DEWEY. I guess I'm kind a wonderin what you might think about dancin.

DARLENE. (*Warming.*) I like dancin just fine.

DEWEY. Me too. I don't know how or nothin but I sure like to watch.

MELVIN. This guy puts the dance floor to shame.

DARLENE. Maybe you could teach me a step or two, Dewey.

MELVIN. (*Referring to* DEWEY.) Hell of a dancer.

DEWEY. Well, my feet're kind a sore. I got planters warts, see?

MELVIN. Now, Dewey that ain't the way to her heart.
DEWEY. (*Exiting.*) I can't dance if my feet hurt.

(BASIL *enters with the bike.* FERRIS *has the pump.*)

BASIL. My damn dogs're dyin.
MELVIN. (*To* DARLENE *as they exit.*) His feet will be fine fore you know it.
BASIL. I bought the damn bike to ride for a change and I end up walkin all over.
FERRIS. Now settle down, Basil.
BASIL. I'm not settlin for nothin! Every time I go to ride the thing, Ferris, the tire goes flat fore you know it.
FERRIS. Now, Basil, . . .
BASIL. Damn bike.
FERRIS. You're gonna upset your system.
BASIL. I've doctored half the cows and kids in the county here, Ferris. I ought to know my own system and my system's piss mad at this tire!
FERRIS. Well, we'll pump her up some and see how she does.
BASIL. Just look at that, will you? A man works his tail off to pay for a thing and just look at it!
FERRIS. Well, the rubber's still good.
BASIL. I tell you, Ferris, I've had it up to here with these Schwinns.
FERRIS. Spokes're alright.
BASIL. Spokes're okay, huh? Well, if it ain't the spokes, it's the rim.
FERRIS. Naw, the rim's lookin fine. If she's not holdin air, it's the tube or your valve.
BASIL. Tubes're pretty costly?
FERRIS. Yeah, but patches're cheap. She needs any work I'll get C.C. right on her.
BASIL. Good worker, is he?

FERRIS. Well, he's new yet, you know.

BASIL. Kind a wet behind the ears, yeah.

FERRIS. And there's two strikes against him, bein born in Kentucky.

BASIL. I'd a thought he's a Hoosier!

FERRIS. Naw.

BASIL. Acts like a Hoosier.

FERRIS. Well, I wasn't too sure when he got here. Hell, I'd hand him a wrench and he'd call it a pliars. Plus, you know he's good lookin.

BASIL. (*Not too happy about the fact.*) Yeah, that's what the wife tells me.

FERRIS. And if there's one thing I've learned in life, Basil, it's that good looking guys make damn awful workers. Back when Bud was just born and the wife was still with us I hired a good lookin kid for a while. Go to put on a headlight, he'd comb his hair in the chrome! Wouldn't get dirty or crawl up under a car.

BASIL. Yeah, those good lookin guys.

FERRIS. They just ain't for shit.

BASIL. Nope.

FERRIS. Course, now C.C. ain't like that. You give him a grease gun you'd think he's in Heaven.

BASIL. I thought those preacher types loved to keep clean.

FERRIS. Well, he does want a wash down the boy.

BASIL. Yeah, they're all the time a dippin, all the time dunkin. Preacher's like a duck around water.

FERRIS. Well he's got another think comin he thinks Bud'll sit still.

BASIL. Who knows? He might do it Ferris. Wouldn't hurt nothin, would it? The boy needs a washin. Will be a hell of a job though.

FERRIS. I know.

BASIL. But if this preacher guy's foursquare you're lucky to have him. What with all the men out a work, you'd think there'd be more half decent help than there is. Not that Dewey and Melvin don't work hard you know.

FERRIS. But they're lazy.

BASIL. They're young yet.

FERRIS. I know.

BASIL. Since the bank's took my tractor I ain't got much choice, Ferris. I need hired help just to keep above water.

FERRIS. Aw, now, Basil, you're fulla shit.

BASIL. Well, I like workin with workers.

FERRIS. (*Handing him the tire pump.*) Then work me this tire, why don't you?

(BASIL *pumps the front tires while* FERRIS *tightens the spokes on the back one.*)

BASIL. I never could run that tractor for nothin you know. The damn thing had too many knobs on it. Too many levers.

FERRIS. You shoulda pulled one and started her up.

BASIL. Naw, tractor's too noisy. Sides, it left big old ruts in my fields.

FERRIS. Never got to your fields.

BASIL. Never got any gas in it. Only bought her cause the wife liked the color.

FERRIS. Least it never got dirty.

BASIL. Nope. The bank took her back. You ask me, they cause all the trouble.

FERRIS. Never had use for a bank.

BASIL. No, the tractors, I mean. Banks can't hurt nothin—they're folded.

FERRIS. Now what's wrong with tractors?

BASIL. Well for starters I hate em. You see, to build the damn things they go rippin the ground up. It's worse'n coal, they go diggin for ore. And to rip out that ore they build more machines—till there's more metal diggin the ground up than men. Then the next thing you know those machines get like rabbits and start makin babies. Little lawn mower machines and hole diggin jobbers. Trench makers . . .

FERRIS. Well diggers . . .

BASIL. Cow milkers . . .

FERRIS. Gets kinda crazy.

BASIL. It gets so a man touches nothin but metal. And metal just don't feel so good to my hands . . . leastways not the way that the earth does.

FERRIS. (*Softly.*) Times ain't what they used to.

BASIL. Well it makes me mad that there's men out of work and they keep right on buildin machines. A man don't work, he can't hold up his head—look his kids in the eye. You take a man's work and you take half the man.

FERRIS. Listen Basil, things're bound to come around, huh?

BASIL. (*Not believing it.*) Yeah.

FERRIS. I'm sayin you gotta want things better or they only get worse, huh?

BASIL. Yeah, Ferris. Yeah, maybe good times're comin. You know they got some fancy kind a manure spreader now. It's in all a them Farm Bureau News things. Biggest damn machine you could dream of. You pull it around, see—and it shits on your fields. (*Pause.*)

FERRIS. Basil, hand me that valve cap, why don't you?

BASIL. The what?

FERRIS. I need the little cap here that fits to your valve. The stems's kind a worn, but if you keep the cap on her you might keep some air in it, Basil.

BASIL. That little cap thing's a part a the tire?

FERRIS. A course it's a part a the tire.

BASIL. Well, I didn't know. I thought it was just there for looks.

FERRIS. Took it off, huh?

BASIL. Can't stand a thing just for looks.

FERRIS. Did you toss it?

BASIL. No, I didn't toss it. I never toss a damn thing. I set it to the shelf in my barn.

FERRIS. Well, take it off a the shelf, put it back on the Schwinn and you'll stop losin air all the time.

BASIL. It ain't just for looks, huh?

FERRIS. Basil, if it's on a Schwinn it's there for a reason.

BASIL. Yeah. Schwinn's a good bike.

FERRIS. Don't make em much better. (BASIL *starts to get on the bike.*) But I wouldn't ride the thing, Basil, till you get the cap on her.

BASIL. Well the sun's full up now. It's a good mornin for walkin.

FERRIS. (*Looking at the sky.*) Looks to be a real nice day.

BASIL. The whole lay a the land looks nice in the mornin.

FERRIS. Yeah.

BASIL. Yep.

FERRIS. Well you stay on those dogs now and walk 'em.

BASIL. Will do.

(BUDDY *and* SHOWERS *enter as* BASIL *walks the bike offstage and* FERRIS *exits up to the garage.*)

BUDDY. Your foots itchin awful?

SHOWERS. No, they kind a smell bad though.

BUDDY. Itchin like crazy, C.C.

SHOWERS. Life's awful tough, ain't it.

(NORMA *enters with a colorful jar of jellybeans.*)

BUDDY. He'll feel better he gets him some jelly beans.

NORMA. Sorry. These beans ain't for sale. You can shop around the Dry Goods all you like, honey, but this candy's stayin right here.

BUDDY. Well he's sick you know, Norma.

NORMA. (*Concerned.*) Oh, what's the matter with you, honey?

BUDDY. (*Sticking his feet up.*) Itchin like nuts. How bout you?

NORMA. Oh, Bud.

SHOWERS. We're hopin you might have some healin salts, ma'am.

NORMA. Best salts in the county. Little fever, little epsom might help you some. A bad rash is a tough thing to shake.

BUDDY. How bout you just give him them jellybeans?

NORMA. Buddy, those beans ain't for sale. This jar a candy means business.

BUDDY. (*Impressed.*) Them're business beans, Norma?

NORMA. The fella that guesses how many're in here gets to take the whole jar home scott free.

SHOWERS. Lucky fella.

NORMA. You wouldn't care to take a guess for yourself? Would you, Mr?

BUDDY. (*Grabs the jar.*) Yeah. Come on, C.C.

SHOWERS. Let me confer with my friend here a moment.

NORMA. It ain't so easy like it looks, I'll tell you that

much right off. I did her once before, but with peanuts.
My niece Darlene, she says, "Oh, Aunt Norma that's sil-
ly," she says, "I could guess how many in a minute." But
I'll tell you those goobers sat here on the counter for a
whole solid year.

SHOWERS. I hear you.

NORMA. You bout ready?

SHOWERS. I think we are, Ma'am.

NORMA. It's a whole lot more that she looks. I had
those goobers just sit here all year.

(SHOWERS *and* BUDDY *guess with no consultation
between them.* SHOWERS *just makes a random
estimate and* BUDDY *throws out the highest number
he knows.*)

SHOWERS. Well, we'd say there's about . . . seven hun-
dred and . . .

BUDDY. Two.

(*Pause.* NORMA *looks like she's just seen a ghost.
very quiet:*)

NORMA. Come again?

SHOWERS. (*Slight pause. Then quietly:*) Seven hun-
dred and two, Ma'am . . .

(*Pause. Then with full conviction of the miracle in
her presense.*)

NORMA. Why, you're that new preacher fella, ain't
you?

BUDDY. Want some candy, C.C.?

NORMA. I been wantin to meet you the whole summer,

Pastor! Lord am I glad that you're here. You should a dropped by the Dry Goods and saw me before. There's all kinds a work to be done. There are back slidin sinners all over this town.

SHOWERS. Ma'am, I just work down the garage.

NORMA. I can see how the Lord's workin through you.

BUDDY. Ain't you hungry, C.C.?

NORMA. You're gonna heal the boy, ain't you? Gonna stop his affliction? (*Covering* BUDDY's *ears.*) Lord knows it ain't gonna be easy.

BUDDY. What?

NORMA. Lord know he could use it.

BUDDY. (*Shaking his head.*) Hey, he can't hear.

SHOWERS. Ma'am, you're just a little mixed up here.

NORMA. I know just what you're doin. You're healin the boy.

SHOWERS. (*Taking charge.*) Here's a dime for the salts, Ma'am, you keep the candy. I got work to do now, so we'll see you.

NORMA. But, Pastor, . . .

SHOWERS. Come on, Bud.

NORMA. (*Calling after them as they exit.*) If you need any help, Pastor, just turn to me. I been prayin for this for years and years now. I've said all along this is what the boy needs.

(GOLDIE *and* LUELLA *enter as if walking down the street or leaving the cafe or something.*)

NORMA. (*Continued.*) The beans—these beans're a sign.

LUELLA. Tastes like plain old candy to me, Norma.

NORMA. Those beans're a sign if ever there was one. That man's got the spirit clean through him.

GOLDIE. But he told me right to my face that he gave up on preachin.

NORMA. You can't toss off the spirit like you toss off a coat. When the Lord sends a sign he means business. It's a blessin, you see. It's a gift the man has.

LUELLA. Now, Norma . . .

NORMA. Don't you "Now, Norma" me. I never seen nothin like it.

GOLDIE. You best rest yourself some.

NORMA. I'm tellin you, Goldie, that man is amazin. He'll bring the whole town to the Lord.

(BUDDY *and* SHOWERS *enter as the women walk* NORMA *offstage. The moon rises during the scene.*)

BUDDY. How come he can't find him no angels, C.C.?

SHOWERS. You been lookin for angels?

BUDDY. Been lookin all over and he can't find em nowheres. You think maybe they's hidin, C.C.?

SHOWERS. Well there's lots of things around you can't lay your eyes on. Now you see the moon risin, don't you?

BUDDY. Yeah.

SHOWERS. Well where do you figure the moon goes in the daytime?

BUDDY. Well he don't recollect it C.C.

SHOWERS. Just because you can't see it doesn't mean it's not there. There's all kinds a things you can't see.

BUDDY. You know who lives up there, don't you? The moon man.

SHOWERS. Does he now?

(JENNIE MAE *enters with a tub of hot water.*)

JENNIE MAE. Sure, he' up there eatin green cheese.

SHOWERS. (*Smiles.*) Kind a hungry now, is he?

BUDDY. Yeah. What do you got in that soup?

JENNIE MAE. Well, it's mainly just salts.

BUDDY. Can he taste it?

JENNIE MAE. I wouldn't taste the stuff, Bud.

SHOWERS. But you're sure more than welcome to touch it.

BUDDY. (*Sensing something is not right.*) You gonna make him?

SHOWERS. No.

BUDDY. He don't wanna touch nothin.

SHOWERS. Well, I'll tell you, my friend, I never seen nothin like it. What we're onto right here is amazin.

BUDDY. Don't make him get wet.

SHOWERS. This ain't just your run a the mill here, my friend.

BUDDY. He ain't gonna go in no water!

JENNIE MAE. Now Buddy . . .

SHOWERS. (*Overlapping.*) This stuff ain't just water.

BUDDY. He can't breathe if you wash him, C.C.!

JENNIE MAE. Just relax . . .

BUDDY. Gonna scream! He's gonna holler!

SHOWERS. (*Forceful.*) Now calm down a little! Just look at this for a second!

BUDDY. He don't need him no bath!

SHOWERS. (*More forceful.*) Now water's usually cold, ain't it, Bud?

BUDDY. He can't breathe in a water!

SHOWERS. Don't go away! I asked you a question! Now answer me, Buddy! I said, ain't water cold? Buddy, ain't water freezin? I always thought that water was cold.

BUDDY. (*Reluctant, keeping his distance.*) Yeah . . .

SHOWERS. Well, I know for a fact that this sure ain't near cold. It ain't cold cause it's warm! This ain't just plain water.

JENNIE MAE. Just look at it, Bud.

SHOWERS. I tell you, my friend, I am absolutely astounded by what's in this bucket.

BUDDY. (*Still keeping his distance.*) What is it!

SHOWERS. What we're onto right here is called . . . itch-juice.

BUDDY. Itch-juice?

SHOWERS. In a manner of speakin.

BUDDY. (*Moving closer.*) What's it do to him, C.C.?

SHOWERS. Well, the wonderful thing about itch-juice, my friend, is it takes the itchin right out a your feet.

BUDDY. Will it hurt him, Jennie Mae?

JENNIE MAE. Folks say it makes you feel better.

SHOWERS. Sure does. I knew a fella way back in Hazard, in fact—had him a horrible case a the rash. Scratchin and itchin, like to drive himself crazy. Till the day he stumbled onto this itch-juice.

BUDDY. It ain't gonna hurt him?

SHOWERS. Bud, there's nothin on earth gonna hurt you.

BUDDY. (*Moving closer, looking in the bucket.*) Kinda gives him the willies all over, Jennie Mae. Got the willies somethin awful, C.C.

SHOWERS. Now, Bud . . .

JENNIE MAE. I'd say Mr. Showers knows just what he's doing.

BUDDY. He ain't feelin so sure he can breathe right no more. (BUDDY *is directly above the bucket. He pulls into himself, very scared. Starting to move away.*) He ain't gonna touch it!

SHOWERS. (*Taking charge.*) Now hold the boat, Bud!

What say you and me make a deal here, pal.

BUDDY. (*Scared to give his word.*) Word a honor C.C.?

(SHOWERS *licks his palm and holds it out. The boy hesitates, decides, they bring their hands together. BUDDY grabs onto* SHOWERS' *hand very tightly—possibly using both hands. As if the preacher can keep him from harm:*)

SHOWERS. Now. There's nothin like singin to put a good man at ease. Lets you forget about anything might be at you, you see, and it settles your insides right down.

(JENNIE MAE *is rolling the boy's pants legs up.*)

BUDDY. You want him to sing, C.C.?

SHOWERS. And by the time you finish we'll have this itchin right out a your feet.

JENNIE MAE. Just relax now . . .

(BUDDY *lets go of* SHOWERS' *hand and leans back, looking straight up at the sky so as not to see the bucket. When he begins to sing his vouce is full of nervous energy. He's as tense and anxious as a child can be, knowing that something is sure to cause him great pain. They begin to wash his feet during the second line of the song. As the water touches him, everything in his voice and body suddenly tense and take on all the fear and terror of the water, as if in great pain.* JENNIE MAE *washes one foot and* SHOWERS *the other:*)

BUDDY.

"You are his sunshine, his only sunshine,
You make him happy when skies are grey.
You'll never know, dear, how much he loves you
Please don't take his sunshine away . . ."

(SHOWERS *immediately leads the boy into the second
     verse and* JENNIE MAE *joins in after a moment.
     They sing softly gently, with reassurance.* BUDDY's
     voice is most prominent still as if in great pain.)

FOOT-WASHERS.
"The other night dear, as he was sleepin,
He dreamt he held you in his arms.
But when he woke, dear, he was mistaken,
So he hung his head and cried . . ."
(*As they sing the final verse the boy's voice relaxes just a
     bit. Growing softer. The lights are changing, form-
     ing a circle around them and framing them—its
     center is the boy's face.*)

FOOT-WASHERS.
"You are his sunshine, his only sunshine,
You make him happy when skies are grey.
You'll never know, dear, how much he loves you.
Please don't take his sunshine away . . ."

(*The lights are fading, the singing has grown gentle.
     The last sound we hear, and we should hear several
     moments of it before the lights go to black, is the
     unamplified sound of water washing again and
     again over the boy's feet.*)

END OF ACT ONE

ACT TWO: THE SKY AND THE WATER

(*Morning. Faint sounds of birds. As the light rises we see* BUDDY *creeping onto the stage, bent low with one hand held out as he tries to befriend a small bird:*)

BUDDY. Ain't you so pretty, huh? Ain't you so pretty. You're the color a the sky. Yes, you are. You want a be up there, now, don't you? In the sun and the wind. Well, hold still, now. Hold still. He ain't gonna hurt you. (SHOWERS *enters as the boy catches the bird.*) You're too little to fly. Shhh, you're alright.

SHOWERS. Is he hurt?

BUDDY. Look at him, C.C. He's little.

SHOWERS. It's an awful pretty bird.

BUDDY. See his feathers?

SHOWERS. Those're blue.

BUDDY. Blue?

SHOWERS. Blue like your eyes.

BUDDY. His eyes is blue?

SHOWERS. Like the bird, like the sky—that's all blue.

BUDDY. Boy. You want a lift him, C.C.? Put him back to his Mama? (BUDDY *climbs on* SHOWERS' *shoulders and they move downstage to the edge of the stage.*)

SHOWERS. Careful, now, pal. You alright?

BUDDY. Yeah. How bout you?

SHOWERS. Oh, you're awful heavy! Now watch yourself up there. You got him?

BUDDY. (*As he places the bird in the tree.*) What color's that?

SHOWERS. That's green.

62

BUDDY. Green? Trees is green. Weeds is green. Grass is green. And birds're blue.

SHOWERS. (*Letting the boy down.*) You're awful smart first thing in the mornin.

(BUDDIE *lies on the stage floor looking up at the trees.*)

BUDDY. Like to live up there with him. His arms turn to wings and his wings turn to feathers.

SHOWERS. How'd you get down?

BUDDY. He'd just fly down, C.C.

SHOWERS. Well, if you're gonna be barnstormin you'd best get your wings out.

BUDDY. Like a bird?

(SHOWERS *holds onto the boy's arms, slowly lifting his upper body until the boy stands on his toes with his arms extended.*)

SHOWERS. Like a bird.

BUDDY. Is he flyin?

SHOWERS. Shut your eyes, now.

BUDDY. Is he flyin?

SHOWERS. If you're willin to fly, pal, I'm willin to witness.

BUDDY. Lift him higher.

SHOWERS. Higher?

BUDDY. Lift him way up the sky! Clear up the sky!

SHOWERS. Higher?

BUDDY. Higher! (BUDDY *runs to a high platform.*)

SHOWERS. (*As if calling a great distance.*) How's the air up there?

BUDDY. Blue!

SHOWERS. Where's Buddy Layman?
BUDDY. He's flyin!
SHOWERS. Flyin!
BUDDY. Flyin clear up the sky! Way up the sky!
SHOWERS. Have you seen Mr. Lindbergh? Any word
from Mr. Lindbergh?
BUDDY. Mr. Who?
SHOWERS. Mr. Lindbergh!
BUDDY. Ain't nobody flyin but birds.
SHOWERS. Any sign a Buddy Layman?
BUDDY. Who's Buddy Layman!
SHOWERS. He's a good boy.
BUDDY. (*Pleased.*) He is?
SHOWERS. He's a smart boy. I know him.
BUDDY. Have you seen Mr. C.C.?
SHOWERS. Mr. Who?
BUDDY. Mr. C.C.?
SHOWERS. Who's Mr. C.C.?
BUDDY. He's a bird!

(SHOWERS *has spread his arms and moved up behind the
     boy. The distance games with their voices stop.*)

SHOWERS. A bird brain, you mean.
BUDDY. Hey, C.C.? You flyin?
SHOWERS. Keep your eyes closed.
BUDDY. (*Amazed.*) You're flyin.
SHOWERS. Want a go higher?
BUDDY. He wants to go where you go, C.C.
SHOWERS. I'm stayin right here with you.
BUDDY. You like it here?
SHOWERS. I like it just fine.
BUDDY. (*Softly.*) You like the wind?
SHOWERS. Feels nice . . .

BUDDY. Feels soft . . .

SHOWERS. That's a nice sort a feelin.

BUDDY. His Mama's soft like the wind. Her voice's soft when he's sleepin.

SHOWERS. That's a dream, my friend.

BUDDY. (*Concerned.*) Is angels a dream?

SHOWERS. Buddy.

BUDDY. How come he can't find her?

SHOWERS. Your Mama's been gone a long time now.

BUDDY. He wants her so bad.

SHOWERS. I know.

BUDDY. If his arms turn to wings and his wings turn to feathers he could find her in the sky, maybe, C.C. (*The boy moves away from* SHOWERS.) If he's flyin he could be with his Mama.

SHOWERS. Buddy, listen to me . . .

BUDDY. (*Overlapping.*) They could fly in the sky, in the wind, in the sun! He could be with his Mama! They could fly and they fly and they fly!

SHOWERS. (*Overlapping from the next to last "fly".*) Your Mama's not here anymore!

BUDDY. He has to find her!

SHOWERS. (*Forceful.*) No! You have to remember! She's left you a father and a sister and there's friends here for Buddy! And they want him and need him and love him! And he isn't a bird—he's a boy! You're a boy. You're a son. You're a brother. And you're a friend.

BUDDY. (*Moved.*) And you like him?

SHOWERS. I like him a lot.

BUDDY. That's somethin, huh?

SHOWERS. You know it is.

BUDDY. Hey C.C.? You know what?

SHOWERS. What?

BUDDY. (*Shakes his hand.*) You're a good guy.

SHOWERS. I am, huh? Well you too!

BUDDY. Buddy is?

SHOWERS. Sure you are.

BUDDY. You know what else he is, C.C.? He's itchin.

SHOWERS. Still itchin?

BUDDY. Right there, C.C. Itchin right there.

SHOWERS. Well, the skin looks a little red yet.

BUDDY. He don't want no more itch-juice.

SHOWERS. You'll never get better if you keep scratchin, Bud.

BUDDY. Well it itches!

SHOWERS. I know — but anytime your legs start to get at you, you say "I'm gonna save this scratch for another time." (SHOWERS *starts to cross away*.)

BUDDY. Hey, C.C.? When's it gonna be another time?

SHOWERS. After you're better.

BUDDY. Is he better now?

SHOWERS. Nope.

BUDDY. Not yet?

SHOWERS. Not quite.

(MELVIN *and* DEWEY *come on left.* DEWEY *is dancing.*
    BUDDY *and* SHOWERS *leave right.*)

MELVIN. You're lookin better.

BUDDY. After while?

SHOWERS. After a while.

DEWEY. After the right foot then the left foot. It's a long step and then a short step. Long step and a short step . . .

MELVIN. Now you're not lookin bad, Dew. But you can't be tippy toe dancin with a girl like Darlene. A girl likes a man to be leadin.

DEWEY. So maybe I want a spin her around, huh? A little razzamatazz?

MELVIN. Dewey, you go tippy toein around her and you're nowhere, you see? Dancin's a damn serious business.

DEWEY. Well, I don't want a be fancy-dancin and get her in trouble.

MELVIN. Now Dewey.

DEWEY. You know what I mean.

MELVIN. Have you been hangin around to the Dry Goods again, Dew? Hey, Dewey.

DEWEY. Yeah, I guess.

MELVIN. What's Norma Henshaw been tellin you?

DEWEY. Nothin much.

MELVIN. Oh, come on, Dew. Dewey?

DEWEY. (*Sudden.*) Says dancin's a sin.

MELVIN. What!

DEWEY. She says it's a sin.

MELVIN. Naw.

DEWEY. Darlene's Aunt says it's right in the Bible. Plain as the day is long! Dancin is sin. S-I-N, sin!

MELVIN. Dancin's just dancin, Dew! It's got nothin to do with the Bible!

DEWEY. I'm on a one way road to you know where, Melvin.

MELVIN. If you want to know about the Bible then go out the garage and have a talk with the Preacher! But you want a know about dancin or drinkin or girls — you stick right here and ask me.

DEWEY. Yeah?

MELVIN. Dew, you name it, I know it. There ain't much I ain't seen.

DEWEY. Well, I'll be.

MELVIN. Listen, Dew. I been around. Here now, you

be you, and I'll be Darlene. Put your arm around me. Hey. Would you knock it off, Dewey? I'm tryin to teach you.

DEWEY. Sorry.

MELVIN. Alright. Now the first rule a dancin is girls're flesh and blood.

DEWEY. I got that much down pretty good.

MELVIN. So you want to keep her close to you. And you don't want a be steppin on her feet, Dew.

DEWEY. Sorry.

MELVIN. Alright. (*They dance across the stage.* MELVIN *calls out the steps like a drill sergeant in a military cadance. Neither of them notice when* BASIL *enters with a pitch fork.*)

MELVIN. Left! Right! Left! Right! Left! Right! Left! Right!

BASIL. (*Overlapping with the last "left!"*) I'm not gonna say you boys're dawdlin around, or goof-offs or do-nothins. And I'm not gonna tell you that you're tryin to cheat me out a the seventy some cents a day that I'm good enough to pay you. I'm just gonna point to that mound a hay over there that somebody, some poor old farmer, spent half his day stackin. And if that hay ain't loaded to the flatbed and hauled to the barn inside an hour — I am more than like to go out and buy me a damn tractor! (BASIL *hands* MELVIN *the pitch fork and stomps off.*)

MELVIN. You know if Basil ever fires us, Dewey, we're gonna have to go find us a job.

DEWEY. I can't hardly breathe without gettin in trouble. I can't romance or dance and now I can't even work right.

(DARLENE, JENNIE MAE, *and* BUDDY *enter. The boy and*

*his sister each have a spoon. They dig for "worms"
and put them in a tin can.*)

DARLENE. Don't let 'em near me.

MELVIN. (*As he and* DEWEY *exit.*) Don't let it get to
you, Dew.

JENNIE MAE. Don't be so prissy, Darlene.

DEWEY. (*Exiting.*) I don't mean to be gettin in trouble.

DARLENE. I'm not about to let em touch me.

BUDDY. How come?

DARLENE. Cause I don't like worms. That's how
come.

JENNIE MAE. Just put em in the can, Buddy.

BUDDY. He is.

DARLENE. It was me, I'd make that preacher dig em
himself.

JENNIE MAE. I don't mind.

DARLENE. Who ever heard of a man askin you out
and then makin you do all the work?

JENNIE MAE. Mr. Showers isn't askin me nowhere,
Darlene. He just said it might be nice to go fishin.

DARLENE. Same thing, Jennie Mae.

BUDDY. (*Dangling a "worm".*) Hey, Darlene.

DARLENE. Jennie Mae!

JENNIE MAE. Buddy!

BUDDY. Just put em in a can.

JENNIE MAE. Just keep diggin and mind your own
business.

DARLENE. It wouldn't bother me so much, see? But
they used to be able to walk.

JENNIE MAE. Worms?

DARLENE. Sure. Worms and snakes both. They could
talk too.

JENNIE MAE. Oh come on.

DARLENE. It's true, Jennie Mae. Don't you guys read the Bible?

BUDDY. Nope, How bout you?

DARLENE. (*Not too happy about the fact.*) Yeah, I gotta learn the whole thing. Like, say I'm sittin at the table and I want seconds on dessert, Aunt Norma says, "Give me a verse first, Darlene." If I didn't know the Bible I'd starve to death, see?

JENNIE MAE. Your Aunt's awful strict.

DARLENE. But I been learnin who Adam and Eve are. You heard a them, ain't you?

BUDDY. Nope.

JENNIE MAE. The first people.

DARLENE. And they're livin in this great big old garden in Europe. And the thing about Eve is she's walkin around pickin berries and junk with no clothes on.

JENNIE MAE. She was naked?

DARLENE. Listen, Jennie Mae, they were like doin it all the time.

JENNIE MAE. They were doin it?

DARLENE. All the time, Jennie Mae.

BUDDY. What're they doin?

JENNIE MAE. Nothin.

BUDDY. Nothin?

DARLENE. All the time, Jennie Mae. That kind a stuff happens in Europe. But like I'm sayin, this snake comes strollin up, see? And he tells her how she's sittin there jaybird stark naked.

BUDDY. She's neked?

JENNIE MAE. Oh, that's crazy, Darlene.

DARLENE. Oh, there's lots crazier stuff'n that in the Bible. Like there's people turnin to stone. One minute they're sittin there just shootin the breeze — and the next thing you know they're all rocks! Lots a wierd stuff.

BUDDY. How come they's rocks?

DARLENE. Cause they ask too many dumb questions.

JENNIE MAE. (*Watching out for her brother.*) Darlene.

DARLENE. So anyway, this business a bein naked really sets God off at the snake, see? Cause with Eve bein so dumb she didn't get in any trouble, but now it's like a whole nother ball game. And God wasn't just mad at this one snake either — he was mad at all a the snakes and all a the worms in the world. So he tells em "From now on you guys're gonna crawl around in the dirt!" God says, "From now on nobody likes you."

JENNIE MAE. God really said that?

DARLENE. Right in the Bible. Later on he gets really mad and floods the whole world out.

JENNIE MAE. You mean he kills em?

BUDDY. With water?

DARLENE. Floods em right under.

BUDDY. Under water?

DARLENE. He makes it keep rainin, see?

BUDDY. God makes it rain? He can't breathe in a water . . .

JENNIE MAE. It's only a story.

DARLENE. It's in the Bible — it's true.

BUDDY. How come God's mad? He ain't done nothin wrong. (BUDDY *runs cross stage as* FERRIS *and* SHOWERS *come out of the garage.*)

JENNIE MAE. It's only a story, Buddy! Wait!

BUDDY. It's gonna rain, C.C.! Gonna rain and it ain't gonna quit, Dad!

FERRIS. Now, slow down —

SHOWERS. Whats a matter?

JENNIE MAE. (*Exiting.*) Why'd you scare him so bad?

DARLENE. (*Following her off.*) I didn't mean to.

BUDDY. Ain't nobody gonna be breathin no more!

FERRIS. Now, Bud—

BUDDY. Gonna rain and it ain't gonna quit! God's makin it rain! Can't you hear him?

SHOWERS. You're alright.

BUDDY. Come on! We gotta hide!

FERRIS. Calm down . . .

BUDDY. We gotta hide!

FERRIS. (*Taking charge, forceful:*) I said calm down a minute and hold your horses, Bud! (*Slight pause. Then gently.*) Now catch your breath, son.

SHOWERS. Nothin's gonna hurt you.

BUDDY. God is!

FERRIS. If God ain't struck down the likes a Herbert Hoover by now, I'd imagine that you're in the clear, Bud.

BUDDY. He is?

FERRIS. (*Exiting.*) I wouldn't worry yourself any.

(BUDDY *is crouched low to the ground rocking back and forth.* SHOWERS *kneels beside him. There is a quiet moment between them as* NORMA *enters with her jar of jellybeans. From her perspective it looks like they are praying.*)

SHOWERS. You alright?

BUDDY. He thinks so.

SHOWERS. Just breathe real easy. There you go. That's a boy.

NORMA. (*To herself.*) Sweet Jesus in Heaven.

SHOWERS. You need to calm down a little.

NORMA. (*Making herself known.*) I knew you could do it! I told the whole town so.

SHOWERS. Beg pardon?

NORMA. I knew that you'd bring that boy to the Lord. I told the Browns and the Bennetts, the Jones and the Seemores—they all know the Lord's workin through you.

SHOWERS. Miz Henshaw . . .

NORMA. Folks come in for miles just to look at this jar! We could set to revivin in no time at'all. Run a real good service.

SHOWERS. Now hold the boat, Ma'am.

NORMA. (*Charging on.*) There'll be singin and savin.

SHOWERS. Would you listen a second?

NORMA. (*Still charging.*) Readin, revivin. You could witness all over the county!

SHOWERS. There's nothin to witness!

NORMA. (*Setting the candy down.*) You don't need to be humble. You can quit at the garage here and take up your Bible—you can do what the Lord wants full time. (*Singing as she exits.*) "What a fellowship, what a joy divine. Leaning on the everlasting arms . . ."

SHOWERS. I like what I'm doin! I don't want a preach! (SHOWERS *calls after her. She should continue to sing once off-stage as if moving farther down the way.*) I spent my whole life tryin to do what the Lord wants! I'm doin for me now, you see?

BUDDY. Hey, C.C.?

SHOWERS. (*Still calling.*) Miz Henshaw!

BUDDY. Whatsa matter?

SHOWERS. God . . . damn her!

BUDDY. (*A little worried.*) Ain't you feelin okay?

SHOWERS. (*Trying to control his anger.*) Just leave me alone, Bud.

(BUDDY *takes a jellybean from the jar and holds it up to* SHOWERS.)

BUDDY. Maybe yiu'll feel better you eat somethin.
SHOWERS. (*Lashing out, knocks the boy's arm away.*) I said leave me alone!
BUDDY. (*As* SHOWERS *exits.*) What's a matter, C.C.?

(NORMA *and* LUELLA *enter with umbrellas as the boy exits. Light sound of a very gentle summer rain. The women set their umbrellas out to dry.* GOLDIE *enters with her tray.*)

NORMA. Just wait'll you hear.
BUDDY. (*Upset.*) Did he do somethin wrong?
LUELLA. That man is amazin.
BUDDY. (*Exiting.*) Hey, C.C.?
NORMA. When you hear what happened not half an hour ago you'll say it's just like I told you all summer.
LUELLA. I'd just as soon tell her myself.
GOLDIE. Let me get you some coffee.
LUELLA. Just half a cup, Goldie. Too much'll give me the skitters.
NORMA. After what she's just been through.
LUELLA. (*Quickly.*) I can tell her myself!
NORMA. She fell right off her bike in the road!
LUELLA. I was maybe half way to Zion when it started to rain, see? So I says to myself as I'm pedalin along—I says, "Luella, the thing to do here is use your umbrella." But to hold the thing up and ride the bike all at once I had to steer with just my left hand, see?
GOLDIE. No wonder you fell.
NORMA. Right down in the road.

LUELLA. And when I go to get up, I can't move!

NORMA. She can't move . . .

LUELLA. First I'd wiggle at my left side and then give a shake at the right. Tried her backwards and forwards and I can't budge an inch!

NORMA. Now, this is the part that's amazin . . .

LUELLA. There I am on my rump in the road, and I've just about given up hope—

NORMA. The part where she meets him.

GOLDIE. Meets who?

NORMA. You know!

GOLDIE. I don't know!

LUELLA. I look up through the rain, Goldie, and who do you think I see comin?

NORMA AND LUELLA. The new preacher!

NORMA. (*Charging on.*) Ain't it amazin, Goldie? Ain't it just like I told you? (*Pause. Quietly:*) You go on, Luella.

LUELLA. So he says to me, "Mrs. Bennett," he says, "Get up off the road, you're just fine." So I says, "I'm not fine—I can't budge, I fell off my blame bike." I says, "if you want a help me, you go get my husband."

GOLDIE. You must a hurt somethin awful.

LUELLA. But the longer I'm talkin the more the preacher keeps starin, till I seen he's starin right in my eyes.

NORMA. Lookin right in her eyes, Goldie—

LUELLA. And it was the funniest sort of a feelin, I tell you—like when he looked in my eyes he saw way down deep inside em. Like he's lookin and seein clean through me.

NORMA. Lookin clean through her, Goldie . . .

GOLDIE. Did he "touch" you?

LUELLA. He says, "I'm gonna hold my hand out here,

Ma'am, and I want you to take it. Just grab hold and we'll boost you right up." And his voice is real quiet and his eyes're real calm, and he says, "Mrs. Bennett, get up." And I'm up . . . !

GOLDIE. (*Amazed.*) And your back was alright?

LUELLA. I tell you, I never felt better. I might a been a little lightheaded, but —

NORMA. Bein lightheaded's a good sign, don't you think?

GOLDIE. You say the pain was all gone?

LUELLA. Goldie I'm as fit as a fiddle. Course now the Schwinn's quite a mess . . .

NORMA. Folks can give up farmin or minin or schoolin or what have you, but a man can't just toss off the spirit. Like a doctor with healin or a singer with singin — when a man's born to preach then he'll preach. I know he don't have a Church and he's not givin sermons but the spirits within him, you see? Don't you remember the Wednesday night meetins and the singins on Sundays — times when the whole town came together. Nearly thirty or forty people together and all singin with one voice on a Sunday. Without a Church here in Zion I don't know where we're goin . . . one day's the same as the days all before . . . but that's gonna change . . . with him layin on hands now and healin folks, ladies — he knows the Lord's with him, you see? We could build us a new Church in no time at'all. The Lord's brought him to town for a reason.

LUELLA. Well, Norma, you surely can witness.

GOLDIE. A Church back in town'd be darn good for business.

NORMA. Be good for us all, don't you think?

LUELLA. I think the sky's gonna clear.

NORMA. I beg pardon?

LUELLA. I says the sky's clearin up some. The sun's pokin through.

NORMA. Now you see there? You see? That's a good sign if ever there was one.

LUELLA. (*Exiting, to herself.*) Zion looks awful nice after a good summer rain.

GOLDIE. (*Same.*) It's a nice town.

NORMA. (*Same.*) And when you think a how long we been with no preacher.

(SHOWERS *and* JENNIE MAE *enter with cane poles, a worm can, etc. A solid green light washes across the stage; the river.*)

JENNIE MAE. How long?

SHOWERS. This long at least.

JENNIE MAE. Oh, C.C.

SHOWERS. Well maybe this long. But I'll tell you that fish was a fighter. By the time we got him to shore and netted alright he liked to bruise up a good dozen men.

JENNIE MAE. Well little sunfish and bluegills about all you can catch here. Fish bottom you might find a carp.

SHOWERS. Sure looks awful pretty.

JENNIE MAE. It's a nice spot for fishin.

SHOWERS. Now look at this, will you? I just here touch bottom. Must get to ten or twelve foot just a couple yards out there.

JENNIE MAE. It gets awful deep towards the middle. Lot a the boys like to come here and swim.

SHOWERS. Now if boys in Indiana are halfway like the boys in Kentucky I wouldn't imagine they bother too much with swim suits.

JENNIE MAE. Yeah, they're the same then.

SHOWERS. (*Smiles.*) I had a feelin they might be. When it comes to swimmin I'm lucky to float. Do a little dog paddlin — that's about it.

JENNIE MAE. I stick to wadin, myself.

SHOWERS. Be happy just dangling my toes in the water. Been a while, I tell you. Too long, I figure.

JENNIE MAE. I thought you fished all the time.

SHOWERS. Well, I used to when I was a kid anyway. But when I had a church I was so full a worry. I never found time to do nothin.

JENNIE MAE. What'd you worry about?

SHOWERS. Everything.

JENNIE MAE. Oh. . . .

SHOWERS. You name it, I worried over it. Like I'd see a family loadin down and taking off for California — they'd say, "Pastor, we ain't got no room for the dog." Well, I'd worry a while, then I'd take the dog. Must had near to a dozen old hounds at once for a while. Good dogs, though. I'd line em all up in the front room and practice my preachin on em. Dogs kinds like bein talked at.

JENNIE MAE. Well you talk real nice.

SHOWERS. I talk too damn much, Jennie Mae.

JENNIE MAE. It's not your fault, C.C. It's the river. My Mama used to say people sit by the water they can't help but be talkin. River's kind a magic like that.

SHOWERS. Your Mama was right.

JENNIE MAE. I don't think she ever liked any place so much as the river. Be down here every other day through the summer And come fall — well you never been here in the fall, but when the leaves start to changin and the air's gettin cooler . . .

SHOWERS. Won't be too long now . . .

JENNIE MAE. And as long as you're here you might as

well stay on through winter. Everythin's nice in the spring.

SHOWERS. Sounds like I might have to stay.

JENNIE MAE. Less you're missin Kentucky.

SHOWERS. Naw. I tell you what I do miss, though, is them dogs.

JENNIE MAE. What'd you do with em all?

SHOWERS. Well, right before I left I gave em all to my kids.

JENNIE MAE. You have kids in Kentucky?

SHOWERS. Oh yeah. Must a had a good couple dozen spread clear cross the county.

JENNIE MAE. Couple dozen?

SHOWERS. Don't get so darned riled, Jennie Mae. They were church kids.

JENNIE MAE. Well I ought to use you for bait, C.C. Showers, but I can't be so mean to the fish.

SHOWERS. You know what those bubbles are on the water there, don't you?

JENNIE MAE. Air, I imagine.

SHOWERS. Those bubbles right there?

JENNIE MAE. Yeah?

SHOWERS. All those millions and trillions of bubbles?

JENNIE MAE. What?

SHOWERS. Fish farts.

JENNIE MAE. Fish farts!

SHOWERS. Jennie Mae, there must be more fish in this river than stars in the sky and we still ain't had a nibble worth a notice.

JENNIE MAE. Well you'll never get a bite with no worm on your hook. Here. Let me put one on for you.

SHOWERS. Naw . . .

JENNIE MAE. I don't mind.

SHOWERS. No, then I'd end up havin to take a fish

off. And don't tell me you'd do that for me too.

JENNIE MAE. Alright, I won't tell you.

SHOWERS. But you would, huh?

JENNIE MAE. If you want.

SHOWERS. (*Setting his pole down.*) Well . . . I'm happy just to sit by the water.

JENNIE MAE. (*Setting her pole down.*) Alright. (*Pause.*)

SHOWERS. You know, Jennie Mae, . . . you know you're awful nice.

JENNIE MAE. Oh . . .

SHOWERS. Yeah you are, and I been meanin to tell you.

JENNIE MAE. You have?

SHOWERS. I sure have. You're real nice, Jennie Mae . . . and you're also . . . (*They are both about ready to kiss.*) . . . real young.

JENNIE MAE. I'm sixteen.

SHOWERS. I know. That's awful young, don't you think?

JENNIE MAE. I don't feel real young.

SHOWERS. Well you are. You don't know how young, Jennie Mae, let me tell you.

JENNIE MAE. My mother was only seventeen when she got married.

SHOWERS. Got married?

JENNIE MAE. Yeah.

SHOWERS. Listen, I think we better head back to the house now.

JENNIE MAE. But we just got here.

SHOWERS. I know, but it's gonna be dark before long and I think we best get home before . . .

JENNIE MAE. Are you tired or somethin?

SHOWERS. Miss Layman, I'm worn to a T.

JENNIE MAE. You want your back rubbed?

SHOWERS. No. No, here now. Let me help you. (*He gives her his hand and helps her stand. They carry their shoes and poles off, etc.*)

JENNIE MAE. (*As he touches her.*) Do you know much about Adam and Eve?

SHOWERS. Yeah . . . yeah I've run into that story before.

JENNIE MAE. You have?

SHOWERS. Yeah, it's a good one alright. But I'm a little more partial to what comes right before. I kind a like all the light the whole story starts out with.

(BUDDY *enters with a lit candle. It is late at night.*)

BUDDY. Ain't they nobody? Ain't they nobody not sleepin? Hey, C.C.? You sleepin? How bout you want a get up? Hey, C.C.? You hear?

SHOWERS. (*Very tired.*) I'm here.

BUDDY. You sleepin?

SHOWERS. Nope.

BUDDY. You awake?

SHOWERS. Nope.

BUDDY. You been sleepin?

SHOWERS. I been tryin, pal.

BUDDY. So's Buddy. He's itchin like nuts. How bout you?

SHOWERS. Bud, there's got to be a cure to all a this itchin . . . (*Yawn.*) . . . and I'll be a happier man when we find her.

BUDDY. How bout you want a rub some goop on him, C.C.?

SHOWERS. Bud, what you got here?

BUDDY. Well, he ain't so sure.

SHOWERS. Bud, this is Wildroot Creamoil. You got your Daddy's hair tonic, pal.

BUDDY. Well, he's itchin.

SHOWERS. Bud, this isn't going to help.

BUDDY. Well it smells good.

SHOWERS. You think maybe you'll get back to sleep if I dab a little on you?

BUDDY. Rub it around his backbones.

SHOWERS. Your back's itchin, huh?

BUDDY. His backbones, his elbones. Itchin like he can't sleep for nothin, C.C.

SHOWERS. Yeah, I know the feelin.

BUDDY. Hey, C.C.? You got one a these? You got a belly buttoner?

SHOWERS. Last time I looked I did.

BUDDY. What's it for?

SHOWERS. As far as I know you're born with it, pal. It's part a the package.

BUDDY. (*Amazed.*) When he's a baby, C.C.? Babies got belly buttoners?

SHOWERS. You're born with all kinds of amazin things. (*Pause.*)

BUDDY. (*Softly.*) Wheres babies come from?

SHOWERS. Well, . . . their Mamas have em.

BUDDY. How come?

SHOWERS. Cause Mamas like having babies, I guess. (*Pause.*)

BUDDY. Hey, C.C.?

SHOWERS. Yeah?

BUDDY. How come she's with Jesus?

SHOWERS. Cause your Mama's in Heaven.

BUDDY. (*Near tears.*) How come he won't give her back?

SHOWERS. Aw, Bud, it just doesn't work that way, is all . . .

BUDDY. Did he do somethin wrong?

SHOWERS. Well, I wouldn't worry yourself too much.

BUDDY. How come?

SHOWERS. Cause we got enough worry with you losin sleep all the time. Now, what do you say we get you Daddy's hair tonic back where it belongs and get you back on into bed, huh?

BUDDY. (*Yawning.*) He ain't so tired, C.C.

SHOWERS. Come on, my friend. It's nearly sunrise. You see in the east there?

(BASIL *and* FERRIS *cross the stage.* FERRIS *has the bike wheel.*)

BASIL. You're yawnin, there, Ferris.

SHOWERS. We're not far from mornin.

BUDDY. Time for breakfast.

SHOWERS. (*Chasing after the boy.*) Time for bed, my friend. Time for sleep.

BASIL. I was wide awake 'fore the sun's in the sky. Lyin to bed and the first thing I thought was, "Today's the day." I rolled over to Luella and I says, "Sugar, I'm gonna pick up the Schwinn."

FERRIS. How's she doin?

BASIL. I don't know. I ain't rode her in two weeks.

FERRIS. No, the wife. I mean the wife.

BASIL. Oh. She's fine. Just fine. How's the boy doin, Ferris?

FERRIS. Bout the same, I guess, Basil.

BASIL. Not still itchin, is he? I better look him over again. I was out along the river tryin to doctor the Simpson boy last week. They had him layed up to bed and takin pills right and left.

FERRIS. What's the boy got the flu?

BASIL. No, he's lovesick. Turns out I walked all the way out there just to have him cry on my shoulder and tell me all about how his dog died. Boy loses a dog it does that sometimes.

FERRIS. Felt the same way when I wrecked my first car.

BASIL. Yeah.

FERRIS. He'll get over it.

BASIL. Well he gets back to the fields and starts bringin in the crops he won't have time to be grievin.

FERRIS. Little hard work'll take care of most things, I guess.

BASIL. What you doin to my tire there, Ferris?

FERRIS. Just workin the spokes.

BASIL. That rim's alright, ain't it?

FERRIS. Yeah, C.C.'s pounded her out pretty nice, pretty even. Move on down there and we'll see how she does. (FERRIS *roles the tire to* BASIL.)

BASIL. Damn thing's always had a wobble to it.

FERRIS. Not bad, though.

BASIL. It'll do. It'll do. I know I'm gettin old fashioned, Ferris, but I look at these damn cars on the road and they're so fast and so noisy . . . I'm like to wish em all away and be done with em. Good for nothin but scarin cattle and kickin the dust up, you ask me. But a bike . . . a bike's a whole nother story. A man gets on his Schwinn and there's no questions asked. Anywhere you want . . . you just peddle along and you're there.

(SHOWERS *and* BUDDY *enter with the rest of the bike.*)

BUDDY. He helped fix her up, Dad. Him and C.C. was workin.

SHOWERS. Bud was in charge a the horses.

FERRIS. The what?

SHOWERS. In charge a holdin his horses.

BASIL. Tough job, huh?

SHOWERS. Oh yeah.

BUDDY. You gonna ride this thing, Basil?

BASIL. You hold your horses, I will. Looks real nice, fellas.

FERRIS. Get this tire on, you're ready to roll. She's got a few miles left in her.

(BUDDY *smears grease on his chest.*)

BASIL. It's a damn wonder she's not more banged up than she is.

SHOWERS. Well, the paint's kind a scratchy.

BASIL. No, the wife. I mean the wife.

SHOWERS. Yeah, she took quite a tumble.

BASIL. Says you helped her out some.

SHOWERS. She's just a little shook is all, Basil.

BASIL. Still, you gave her a hand.

SHOWERS. Just helped her up.

BASIL. Well damn it! Can I thank you or not?

FERRIS. (*As* BASIL *and* SHOWERS *shake hands.*) For a good lookin fella he's alright, huh?

BUDDY. (*Turns to the men, and is now covered with grease.*) Would you look at that boy? He can't keep clean for nothin. He's got grease on his belly, his backbones, . . . he's got grease all over him.

BASIL. Feels good to the skin, huh?

BUDDY. Don't wipe the grease off him!

BASIL. Hold still, now! I want another look at you, boy.

BUDDY. How come?

BASIL. Cause you're so pretty.

BUDDY. (*Pleased, allowing him to look.*) He is?

FERRIS. Sure. Runs in the family.

BASIL. Course, your Dad's an exception.

BUDDY. Doodle bugs're pretty.

FERRIS. Yeah.

BUDDY. Jennie Mae's pretty, too.

SHOWERS. She sure is.

BASIL. (*Concerned.*) Ferris, you ain't touched this boy, have you?

FERRIS. Kind a hopin it'll clear with the seasons.

BASIL. I don't blame you for hopin, but that ain't gonna cure him. Ferris, it's spread somethin awful! On his neck, in his scalp. Another week or two here it's gonna spread to his eyes. Now I told you to wash him!

FERRIS. I know, Basil.

BUDDY. Don't make him get wet.

BASIL. If you don't keep him clean it's gonna spread through his system.

BUDDY. You ain't gonna wash him.

BASIL. Well, Bud, it's the only cure for ringworm I know.

BUDDY. (*Running off.*) He ain't gonna go in no water!

FERRIS. Hey Bud . . . !

BASIL. You fellas're messin with these salts and this skin lotion and it ain't gonna cure a damn thing. You can't cure him a ringworm by puttin things on him. It's under the skin, don't you see?

SHOWERS. Now, hold on a minute. I can't see what you're talkin.

BASIL. I'm talkin the same damn thing I've told Ferris all summer. Warm water and lotions make the pores open up, and once the skin opens that ringworm'll head for high ground. but cold water draws the skin tight, don't you see? If the ringworm can't breathe, he don't bite . . . he don't bite, you don't itch. I'm not sayin it's easy the way the boy is, but if you'll just keep him clean he'll be fine.

FERRIS. (*Under* SHOWERS' *glare.*) Well, damn it, C.C., I can't take the boy's screamin.

SHOWERS. Why didn't you say somethin, Ferris?

FERRIS. You have to think how I feel when the boy's around water.

SHOWERS. You know how to help him and don't bother to tell me?

FERRIS. The boy gets near water and he's screamin and cryin — it just sets off my mind, don't you see?

SHOWERS. I been the whole summer here, Ferris!

FERRIS. You're not the boy's father, not family — you just work here is all!

SHOWERS. You just leave the boy go!

FERRIS. I'm tired of you tellin me what to do all the time!

SHOWERS. Well I'm tired a doin it all, Ferris!

FERRIS. Don't you understand? The boy's mother died in the water! My wife in the water. I was there.

SHOWERS. I don't care about your wife! I care about the boy!

FERRIS. I don't need you to push me!

SHOWERS. Well I'm gonna push you!

FERRIS. Then you can get to hell on down the damn road! We got along just fine before you, we can get on without you! You hear me?

SHOWERS. I hear you!

FERRIS. Well I'm sorry!

SHOWERS. (*Quietly.*) So am I, Ferris.

FERRIS. (*Throws down a rag.*) Well damn it all! (*Pause. Then with control:*) I mean I'm sorry . . . I lose my damn temper too easy.

SHOWERS. I know the feelin . . .

FERRIS. Sometimes a man says things, he doesn't think what he's sayin.

SHOWERS. Sometimes a man's a little too pushy.

FERRIS. Yeah.

SHOWERS. Yeah. I guess I'm just pushy by nature. (*Pause.* SHOWERS, *lost in thought, is spinning one of the bike tires.*)

BASIL. Well. Uh, what do you say we give a push at this bike, fellas?

(SHOWERS *and* FERRIS *turn the bike upright.*)

FERRIS. I got her.

SHOWERS. There you go.

FERRIS. Listen, Basil, I thank you.

BASIL. I'm no doctor, Ferris, but I know what I know. And my advice is to try and relax. If I hollered like you boys I'd give myself the heart failure.

FERRIS. You got your balance now don't you?

BASIL. I'm fine. Just give me a little push is all.

SHOWERS. There you go, cowboy.

BASIL. Not too hard now, damn you!

FERRIS. Take her easy there, Basil.

SHOWERS. Be careful! (*They watch* BASIL *ride off stage. Pause. Then:*)

FERRIS. Well you got any idea how to go about this whole thing?

SHOWERS. Guess we got him in warm, we can get him in cold.

FERRIS. Can't tie the boy up.

SHOWERS. Nope.

FERRIS. And he's tough to hold down.

SHOWERS. Yep.

(JENNIE MAE *and* BUDDY *enter as the men exit.*)

JENNIE MAE. You got yourself all wrapped up in knots, Bud.

BUDDY. Well he was tryin to tie em.

JENNIE MAE. Since when did you start wantin shoes on your feet?

BUDDY. C.C. says he's supposed to keep his dogs in em.

JENNIE MAE. Why's that?

BUDDY. Cause his dogs a got ringworm. Plus he's got her all over the rest of him. Want a see?

JENNIE MAE. No. Now hold still a second. (JENNIE MAE *starts working at getting* BUDDY's *shoe off and his pants legs rolled up.*)

BUDDY. Hurry up, Jennie Mae. S'gonna rain.

(SHOWERS *and* FERRIS *enter and go to the well. The preacher should draw the water from the well, the well light shining faintly.* BUDDY *doesn't notice them yet.*)

FERRIS. Strange sort a day, ain't it?

SHOWERS. Sky's changin, Ferris.

BUDDY. How come, Jennie Mae?

FERRIS. There's a wind risin fast.

BUDDY. How come you're rollin his pants up?

JENNIE MAE. Settle down, Bud.

BUDDY. Ain't you puttin his boots on?

JENNIE MAE. We'll get your shoes back on in a minute or two.

(SHOWERS *pours the well water into a large bucket.* BUDDY, *hearing it, turns and sees the men.*)

BUDDY. Hey! Hey . . . what you guys doin? What you got in that bucket?

SHOWERS. We're gonna try and fix you up, pal.

BUDDY. He says what's in a bucket, C.C.? Can't you hear? (*He realizes.*) Hey . . . hey, they's water in there. Dad?

SHOWERS. Come on, Bud.

(BUDDY *runs to his father as* SHOWERS *goes for him.*)

BUDDY. Dad!

FERRIS. Son, you're gonna be fine.

BUDDY. What you guys doin? Don't make him get wet.

SHOWERS. You're gonna have to sooner or later. (*They pull him towards the bucket. It's a real struggle.* JENNIE MAE *is waiting there with a rag.*)

BUDDY. C.C., he thunk you's his pal! Leave him go!

FERRIS. You're alright!

BUDDY. Leave go of him, Dad! He can't breathe in a water!

JENNIE MAE. Calm down!

BUDDY. Jennie Mae, make em stop! Ain't no air in a water! Leave him go! Leave him go! He can't breathe!

SHOWERS. It's not gonna hurt you! (*They nearly have his feet in the bucket.*)

BUDDY. (*Exploding.*) His Mama's in a water! His Mama! His Mama! Leave him go! He can't breathe! (FERRIS *lets go and* BUDDY *breaks loose.*) Leave him go! (BUDDY *runs off.*)

SHOWERS. Buddy!

JENNIE MAE. Buddy, wait!

SHOWERS. Hey, Bud!

JENNIE MAE. (*Pause. Softly.*) He'll be back soon.

SHOWERS. Buddy—!

JENNIE MAE. (*To her father.*) There's a storm comin.

SHOWERS. Bud—!

JENNIE MAE. Daddy, did you hear me? There's a storm blowin in. He'll be home before long.

SHOWERS. (*Exiting.*) He's in the woods, I guess.

(MELVIN *and* DEWEY *enter, watching the sky.*)

DEWEY. Over those trees there.

JENNIE MAE. He'll be home. (*She exits.* FERRIS *exits after a moment.*)

MELVIN. I never saw clouds like that.

(SHOWERS *can be heard calling "Buddy" at regular intervals from off stage throughout the storm collage.*)

LUELLA. (*Entering with* GOLDIE.) It's gonna rain soon.

NORMA. (*Entering with* DARLENE.) It's fixing to rain awful hard, dear.

DEWEY. Would you look at that sky?

GOLDIE. You'll have to wait out the storm to get home.

MELVIN. Awful dark clouds.

DARLENE. I never saw the sky so full before.

LUELLA. It's been a good summer for rain.

GOLDIE. Nice summer.

NORMA. Are the windows closed?

BASIL. (*Enters and joins his farmhands.*) Are the tools in?

DARLENE. I think so.

MELVIN. Yeah, they're in.

GOLDIE. Gonna storm most the night I'm afraid.

NORMA. Would you listen to that wind?

LUELLA. It's the season for storms.

DARLENE. I can't sleep when it's stormin.

GOLDIE. (*Exiting with* LUELLA.) Best get inside for the sky splits wide open.

NORMA. You'll be alright.

BASIL. I haven't seen the sky like this in years and years.

DARLENE. I never heard the wind so loud before.

DEWEY. Be lightnin and thunder.

MELVIN. Comin soon don't you think?

NORMA. (*Exiting with* DARLENE.) You'll be fine in the house.

BASIL. Won't be long now, boys. We best get inside.

(BUDDY *is heard calling "Mama" off stage as the men exit. Sound of thunder crashing and wind and rain breaking loose intermixed with the boy and the preacher calling.*)

BUDDY. (*Entering.*) Mama—! Mama, the air's all turnin to water! All the air's turned to water! He can't find him no air! Mama—!

SHOWERS. (*Entering.*) Buddy—?

BUDDY. Mama—?

SHOWERS. Buddy, it's alright!

BUDDY. He can't breathe!

SHOWERS. You're alright now, Buddy!

BUDDY. (*Moving away from* SHOWERS.) No, he can't find her! Can't find him no air!

SHOWERS. Buddy, listen to me!

BUDDY. Mama!

SHOWERS. Listen!

BUDDY. The air's all turnin to water!

(*As* SHOWERS *tries to make the boy understand they*

wrestle around the stage. BUDDY *fights for all he's worth.*)

SHOWERS. Hold still and listen!

BUDDY. Leave him go!

SHOWERS. It's the rain! Not the water!

BUDDY. Leave go of him!

SHOWERS. No! You're gonna understand, Buddy! You're gonna figure this out if we have to stay here all night!

BUDDY. He can't breathe!

SHOWERS. You can breathe!

BUDDY. Leave him go! Leave him go! He can't find him no air!

SHOWERS. For a guy who can't breathe you're pretty strong! Now hold still! Hold still and listen!

BUDDY. He can't find her!

SHOWERS. You're not underwater—

BUDDY. Mama—?

SHOWERS. You're not in the water!

BUDDY. Mama!

SHOWERS. Can't you understand? You can breathe!

BUDDY. He has to find her!

SHOWERS. (*Exploding.*) What do I have to do to you damn it? You're not gonna find your Mama here, Buddy! She's dead don't you see, Buddy! Gone!

BUDDY. It ain't his fault, C.C.! Leave him go!

SHOWERS. No!

BUDDY. Leave go of him!

SHOWERS. No!

BUDDY. It ain's his fault how the water took his Mama!

SHOWERS. No! It's not your fault, Buddy! It's nobody's fault!

BUDDY. It ain't!

SHOWERS. No, it ain't!

BUDDY. It ain't Buddy's fault!

SHOWERS. It's not your fault, Buddy!

BUDDY. It ain't Buddy's fault! It ain't Buddy's fault! It ain't, it ain't, it ain't Buddy's fault . . . (*He repeats himself, crying.*)

SHOWERS. (*After a pause. Softly.*) It's nobody's fault.

BUDDY. (*Softly.*) It ain't?

SHOWERS. No.

BUDDY. God took her.

SHOWERS. That's not your fault, Buddy.

BUDDY. God's mad!

SHOWERS. He's not mad!

BUDDY. He's makin it rain!

SHOWERS. Now, Buddy—

BUDDY. God's mad at him, C.C.!

SHOWERS. It rains cause it's water!

BUDDY. (*Accusing.*) It storms!

SHOWERS. Cause it's water! It rains so the plants can grow! It rains so the birds have somethin to drink! It rains because it's water, Buddy! That's what water does!

BUDDY. It does?

SHOWERS. Yeah, that's all it does. Now breathe.

BUDDY. No.

SHOWERS. Breathe!

BUDDY. He ain't gonna.

SHOWERS. You been breathin all along, pal! You might just as well face the fact and get her over with.

BUDDY. He ain't gonna breathe! You can't make him!

SHOWERS. You're breathin right now.

BUDDY. No, he ain't.

SHOWERS. Yeah, you are.

BUDDY. Nope!

SHOWERS. Are you ready?

BUDDY. What you gonna do to him, C.C.?

SHOWERS. We're gonna breathe.

BUDDY. But he can't breathe! (SHOWERS *takes a huge breath and holds it in. Pause.*) Hey, C.C.! It's rainin! He can't breathe in a rain! (BUDDY *becomes concerned for* SHOWERS *well-being.*) Hey, C.C.? You okay? (*He shakes him.*) You alright? Hey, C.C.? (BUDDY *takes a huge breath and holds it.* SHOWERS *immediately exhales.*)

SHOWERS. Now we're gettin somewhere. Feels pretty good, don't it, Bud? Hey, Bud? Buddy, listen. You're best to let out the old and take in some new, pal. (BUDDY *exhales, gasping for air.*) Now what'd you just do?

BUDDY. He breathed. Can't you see him?

SHOWERS. Now let's try her once more. You ready? One, two, three—breathe! (*They take a huge breath together, then another and another and so on—almost like the sound of a train starting up, until they're both breathing along at full tilt.*) You're doin pretty good, pal!

BUDDY. He is?

SHOWERS. Doin fine. Now the wonderful thing about breathin is you can't help but do it all the time, Bud.

BUDDY. He can't?

SHOWERS. Even when you're sleepin you're pretty busy breathin.

BUDDY. When he's sleepin?

SHOWERS. All the time, Bud. Even in the rain.

BUDDY. No siree, C.C.

SHOWERS. Buddy.

BUDDY. What?

SHOWERS. It's rainin.

BUDDY. It's rainin?

SHOWERS. It's lettin up some but it's still rainin.

BUDDY. (*Sudden.*) He can't breathe!

SHOWERS. You can breathe, you are breathin, and you're gonna keep breathin!

BUDDY. In a rain? He's gonna breathe in a rain?

SHOWERS. If there's one thing you are, Bud, it's an A-Number-One breather. Word a honor.

BUDDY. (*Taking it to be a pact.*) Word a honor, C.C.? (*They rub palms together.*)

SHOWERS. Word a honor.

BUDDY. Hey, C.C., you know what? He ain't itchin so bad.

SHOWERS. You know why don't you?

BUDDY. Cause he's breathin!

JENNIE MAE. (*Calling from off stage.*) Buddy—?

SHOWERS. I got a sneakin suspicion it's not just cause you're breathin, but because you been breathin while rollin around in all this rain.

JENNIE MAE. (*Closer.*) Buddy—?

BUDDY. Over here, Jennie Mae! Him and C.C.'re breathin!

JENNIE MAE. Oh, Bud, I been lookin for you half the night, little brother!

BUDDY. (*As she hugs him.*) He can breathe in a water, Jennie Mae. How bout you?

JENNIE MAE. (*To* SHOWERS.) Are you sure he's alright?

SHOWERS. Looks fine to me.

JENNIE MAE. (*Crossing to* SHOWERS.) Like to worry me to death, you two.

SHOWERS. Oh, Jennie Mae.

BUDDY. You guys gonna sweet-talk awhile? You want him to maybe go itch somewheres else?

JENNIE MAE. Buddy Layman.

BUDDY. He's itchin like nuts! His arm pitters, his

backbones . . . (*Slight pause, amazed.*) Cept his dogs ain't itchin.

SHOWERS. That's cause your dogs're in a puddle a water, my friend.

(BUDDY *squats down and splashes some of the "puddle" in his arm pits.*)

JENNIE MAE. Buddy, what're you doin?

BUDDY. Puttin some a this puddle in his pitters. Feels good.

SHOWERS. Listen, you best find your dad and tell him we'll be down to the water.

JENNIE MAE. Right now?

SHOWERS. Go on. We'll be fine.

JENNIE MAE. Well can't you wait for us, C.C.? It won't take me long.

SHOWERS. Go on now. And stop lookin so worried.

JENNIE MAE. You two be careful. (*She exits.*)

BUDDY. He is.

SHOWERS. Come on, pal.

BUDDY. Where we goin?

SHOWERS. (*Walkin past the boy.*) We're gonna try and make you better.

BUDDY. Hey, C.C.—ain't you gonna carry him?

SHOWERS. Aw, Bud, my back's awful wore out.

(NORMA *enters with* DARLENE *and* DEWEY *in tow as* BUDDY *and* SHOWERS *exit. The young folks are slightly spiffed up.*)

NORMA. I am worn through and through with your stories, Darlene. I know you two been off dancin all night. I got eyes. I can see what you're up to.

DEWEY. But, Miz Henshaw—

NORMA. Not a word out a you, Dewey! You got no room to talk after taking my little girl where you been.

DARLENE. But it was beautiful, Aunt Norma. There was decorations and posters and those little toilet paper flower things.

DEWEY. And a band that played songs like they're right off the radio.

DARLENE. It weren't nothin sinful at'all.

NORMA. Dancin is sinful as sinful could be! I thought I could trust you, Darlene.

DARLENE. I'm sorry, Aunt Norma.

NORMA. You kids're gonna be sorry when you talk to the preacher.

DEWEY. But, Miz Henshaw—

JENNIE MAE. (*Calling from off stage.*) Miz Henshaw—

NORMA. Come on.

JENNIE MAE. (*Entering.*) Miz Henshaw! Have you guys seen my Dad?

NORMA. We're marchin straight out the garage to have a talk with the preacher.

JENNIE MAE. Well Mr. Showers is down to the river.

NORMA. The river?

JENNIE MAE. If you see my Dad tell him Buddy's with C.C. and they're both to the water. (JENNIE MAE *runs off.*)

NORMA. Well bless me sweet Jesus. You find that man, Dewey. You find Ferris' Layman if it takes you all mornin and you tell his boy's found the Lord. You hear me?

DEWEY. I'll fetch him.

NORMA. Well go on! Get a move on! (DEWEY *runs off.*) And as for you, Darlene—sneakin out of the house and carousin all night — I never been so ashamed in my life.

DARLENE. I didn't mean to make trouble.

NORMA. I want you to make a B-line for home and get out a that dress. I can't be bringin you to a baptizin in somethin you look like you were born in and been growin into ever since. (*They exit as* BUDDY *and* SHOWERS *enter.* SHOWERS *has the boy on his back. The river light comes up full force.*)

SHOWERS. Aw, Bud, you're gettin awful heavy.

BUDDY. You think he's a fatso?

SHOWERS. I think you're just growin.

BUDDY. Like a weed?

SHOWERS. (*Setting the boy down.*) To say the least.

BUDDY. (*Seeing the river.*) Hey, C.C. — you ain't gonna stick him in that river water?

SHOWERS. You still itchin?

BUDDY. Well he ain't so sure no more . . .

SHOWERS. Now just look at it a second. Come on, Bud. It's not gonna hurt you. You see, the river is more or less like the rain.

BUDDY. Kind a gives him the willies all over, C.C.

SHOWERS. No, now just try and touch it. (SHOWERS *dips his hand into the river and brings up a cupped hand full of water. He pours a little into* BUDDY'S *hand.*) Put a little in your hand. That's a boy.

BUDDY. S'like the rain?

SHOWERS. It's just water. (*He tosses the rest of his handful up in the air.*) You see how it falls?

BUDDY. (*Tossing his handful.*) Like the rain.

SHOWERS. Only there's a little more of it.

BUDDY. Yeah . . .

SHOWERS. Now what do you say we get that shirt of yours off?

BUDDY. Well he ain't so hot with his buttons.

SHOWERS. Stop scratchin a second and I'll help you.

BUDDY. You want him to get neked, C.C.?

SHOWERS. I'd imagine your shirt's close enough. The river's awful pretty this mornin, ain't it?

BUDDY. What color's that? S'that green, C.C.?

SHOWERS. There's all kinds of colors in the water here, pal. See the trees up above. See the leaves changin colors?

BUDDY. How come?

SHOWERS. Cause that's what leaves do in the fall.

BUDDY. You gettin neked?

SHOWERS. Just pullin my boots off.

BUDDY. Your dogs itch?

SHOWERS. Bud, a little water'll do me good, I imagine.

BUDDY. You sure that's like rain?

SHOWERS. Just about. (*He dips his feet in.*) Woooeeee! S'little colder'n I expected . . .

BUDDY. You okay?

SHOWERS. You stay right where you are and watch how I'm wadin. You want a splash it around on you a little. Get yourself used to it some. (*Freezing.*) Feels pretty good, Bud. Real nice . . .

BUDDY. He's like to maybe go find him some breakfast, C.C.

SHOWERS. No. Now just get your feet in for starters. That's all I'm askin. If it's too cold we'll hold off awhile.

BUDDY. Just his dogs is all?

SHOWERS. Just your dogs for starters.

BUDDY. (*Tentatively lets* SHOWERS *dip his feet in.*) Wooooeeee, C.C.! S'freezin!

SHOWERS. Move em around some. (SHOWERS *has* BUDDY *standing in the shallow of the river now.*)

BUDDY. S'awful cold!

SHOWERS. S'awful nice.

BUDDY. Boy oh boy oh boy oh boy oh boy oh boy . . .

SHOWERS. (*Slight overlap.*) Keep movin. That's a boy. There you go.

BUDDY. How you doin?

SHOWERS. I'm doin fine, pal. Feelin dandy.

BUDDY. You gonna wash him all off?

SHOWERS. You warmin up some?

BUDDY. Well he's tryin.

SHOWERS. Alright. (SHOWERS *lifts a handful of water and puts it over the boy's head.*)

BUDDY. Go easy, C.C.! Easy!

SHOWERS. (*Using less water, just a little.*) S'that better?

BUDDY. Hey, C.C.?

SHOWERS. Yeah?

BUDDY. He's a wonder.

SHOWERS. You are, huh? Well what are you a wonder about, Bud?

BUDDY. You think his Mama's okay?

SHOWERS. I figure your Mama's in heaven. (BUDDY *slips just a touch.*) Whoa now! You stick right here close by me.

BUDDY. He is.

SHOWERS. You want to feel your way along the bottom, you see.

BUDDY. Yeah . . . you been to heaven?

SHOWERS. Well, Bud, to tell you the truth I been a little too busy bein here to be much a any place but here.

BUDDY. Well where's heaven at?

SHOWERS. Let me think for a second.

BUDDY. S'in the sky?

SHOWERS. Not exactly . . .

BUDDY. You still thinkin?

SHOWERS. I'm tryin. I guess you could say that heaven's where you are when you ain't here no more.

BUDDY. When you ain't here no more . . .

SHOWERS. Like your Mama.

BUDDY. She's gone.

SHOWERS. Well that's heaven.

(NORMA, DARLENE, GOLDIE, *and* LUELLA *begin to sing "Shall We Gather At The River" off stage. They sound as if they're way in the distance and moving very gradually closer.*)

BUDDY. Hey, C.C. Listen. You hear it?

SHOWERS. What's that?

BUDDY. The river. S'talkin.

SHOWERS. The water, you mean? The waves?

BUDDY. S'talkin, C.C.!

SHOWERS. Well what's it sayin to you, Bud?

BUDDY. Well . . . he don't know.

SHOWERS. Who doesn't know?

BUDDY. He don't.

SHOWERS. (*Pressing.*) Who don't?

BUDDY. Him! Him, C.C.! Can't you hear?

SHOWERS. Yeah, I hear him. You're a pretty good guy, Bud. You know that?

(*The Women are still off, but very close.*)

WOMEN.
"Shall we gather at the river,
Where bright angel feet have trod;
With its crystal tide forever,
That flows by the throne of God?

Yes, we'll gather at the river,
The beautiful, the beautiful river.
Gather with the saints at the river,
That flows by the throne of God —" (*Etc.*)

(BUDDY *and* SHOWERS *totally overlap the singing.*)

BUDDY. Hey. Hey, C.C. — how come they's singin?
SHOWERS. It's alright. (*He calls to the women though they're still off stage.*) Hey, ladies? Ladies, we're trying to wash here, you understand?
BUDDY. He likes it in a water.
SHOWERS. (*To himself.*) What're they doin? (*He calls.*) Hey, ladies? We'd like to be alone here, you see?

(*The women enter up high. They're singing very loud. The song should continue at high volume behind all the dialogue.*)

NORMA. I brought em, Pastor Showers! We're all here to witness!
SHOWERS. We'd like to be alone here.
NORMA. We're here for the baptizin, Pastor!
SHOWERS. This isn't a baptizin!
NORMA. Praise God, the Lord's with him! (*She goes back to singing full force.*)
SHOWERS. I'm just washing the boy. Don't you see?

(*The women sing even louder.* NORMA *acts as a song leader of sorts. As* SHOWERS *loses his temper he lets go of the boy's arm.* BUDDY, *enjoying himself immensely and thinking he can breathe in water, moves away from* SHOWERS *and the women.* SHOWERS *has his back to the boy as he rages at the women.*)

SHOWERS. (*Continued.*) Would you stop singin and listen? This is nothing to do with the Church or the spirit! I'm done with the Church! Would you listen? Stop singin and listen!

BUDDY. He can breathe in a water!

SHOWERS. I'm not gonna baptize him, damn it! Don't make me a preacher!

BUDDY. He's breathin! (BUDDY *steps into the deepest area of the river and is suddenly underwater. At the same moment a sound of something representing underwater silence is heard—very loud, a sort of wail. Wind run at half speed and mixed with a little water sound works pretty well. All action immediately takes on the water's perspective and shifts to extreme or film-like slow motion. The preacher is yelling at the women. No one notices* BUDDY *underwater. When the boy rises the action suddenly shifts into normal stage speed and sound. The sound effects shifts off momentarily.*) C.C.!

SHOWERS. (*Overlapping.*) Would you listen to me!

(BUDDY'S *immediately back underwater and the sound effect and slow motion resume.* JENNIE MAE *enters in slow motion, looking over the water, and sees* BUDDY *as he rises for the second time.*)

BUDDY. Mama—!

JENNIE MAE. Buddy—!

(*The boy is immediately back under water, and the sound effect is immediately up again.* SHOWERS *turns as* JENNIE MAE *screams and sees the boy is missing. He goes underwater and searches the river bottom for the boy.* BUDDY, *as if fighting the current, is slipping several yards cross stage and fighting to pull himself back.* SHOWERS *searches the river bottom on his belly, pulling himself along the raked stage, feeling along before him with his hands. When he needs air he pulls himself back towards the women, and bursts from the water.*)

NORMA. Thy Kingdom come! Thy will be done!
JENNIE MAE. (*Overlapping.*) My brother! My brother!

(*As* SHOWERS *goes under again the sound comes back up as before.* GOLDIE *is holding* JENNIE MAE *back from the water.* NORMA *is praying as if it will somehow save the boy. As the preacher rises again:*)

NORMA. Forgive us our tresspasses as we forgive!
GOLDIE. (*Overlapping.*) It's alright!
JENNIE MAE. (*Overlapping.*) My brother!

(SHOWERS *goes under water immediately and the sound comes back on. He searches, nearly reaching the boy. He stays under as long as he can. The boy dies as the preacher pulls himself towards shore. As he rises:*)

NORMA. And the glory forever and ever! (*Slight pause.*) Amen.

(*There is only the sound of the gently flowing water and* SHOWERS *coughing, gasping for air. He pulls himself part way on to the river bank and turns, looking over the water.*)

SHOWERS. Oh, my God. Oh my God my God my God . . .

(*The dulcimer begins to play "Amazing Grace" slowly, one string, one note at a time—solemn and grieving in its music. The women and the preacher hold their tableau.*)

SECOND ELEGY

(*The river fades as two pin spots rise on either side of the stage, BASIL and DEWEY entering. Except for the possibility of a morning sky behind them, theirs are the only lights on stage. They speak directly to the audience, as in the beginning. The dulcimer grows strong and full behind them.*)

BASIL. And like a slate wiped clean or a fever washed away where there was fire to the sky now there's nothin. Where there was clouds there's just blue and the sun.

DEWEY. His only son gone and it's me who brings the word when I find Ferris Layman that mornin. I'd run to the river and I seen the boy there and I run like the wind for his father! I says, "Ferris . . . I'm sorry." And he don't move and don't speak. I says, "Your son, he's passed on beyond us."

BASIL. Buddy Layman's dead, don't you see? When he said it would rain we layed our fields in rows and we knew it would be a good season.

DEWEY. And now we harvest the fields and we turn the ground over.

BASIL. Turn the earth to the earth like a child to his mother. And we think a the boy and we call it a blessin. We turn to each other and we call it a blessin.

(*The lights fade to black as the dulcimer strikes a final chord.*)

A NOTE ON THE BOY

Buddy can be played as either fourteen or seventeen years old, depending on the actor. If he's played as seventeen then several line changes are in order. His sister should call him "big brother" instead of "little brother" — or she should simply call him "Buddy" when "big brother" seems inappropriate. In the Cafe scene in the first act (*page 33*) the lines should read so that Goldie says, "He's only a boy, Ferris!" and Ferris responds, "The boy's seventeen! When I was his age I cussed all the time!", etc. Finally, in Ferris's monologue in the first act (*page 44*) he would say, "I wasn't married a year and she give me a son. I was just gettin used to a wife." His next line would then read, "then the girl came along."

Buddy's central trait is his innocence, his vulnerability. He shouldn't have too much of a speech impediment, though his speech should be hesitant when he's discovering something or confused or frightened. His gestures, his walk, and his whole physical attitude should reflect both an emotional and intellectual frustration, or more simply, sometimes a coordination problem. Clinically speaking, he isn't modeled on any specific emotional or physical disorder.

COSTUME PLOT

BUDDY LAYMAN
Overalls — very dirty
Blue plaid flannel shirt — very dirty
Black lace up ankle high boots — very dirty
(must muddy body including hair — nightly)

JENNIE MAE
Pale blue old cotton floral 20's style dress
Slip
Blue checked half-apron
Brown leather tie shoes
Off-white cotton socks
Cut-off long johns under dress

FERRIS
Pale blue striped shirt w/grease stains
Suspenders
Leather belt
Baggy jeans
Cap
Cotton socks
Brown leather ankle high boots
Pocket watch
Blue patterned hankerchief

C.C. SHOWERS
Pale blue shirt w/pattern
Brown striped tie
Matching suit coat & vest-brown
Brown suit trousers (not matching vest and coat)
Black ankle high lace up boots
Brown felt fedora
Off-white man's hankerchief
(*Everything should look very old*)

NORMA
Rusty brown and cream floral 20's style cotton dress
Black tie "sensible shoes"
Gold-striped faded work smock
No stockings
Gold pin on collar

DARLENE
Pale yellow cotton 20's style dress
Pink hand knit cardigan
Brown flat shoes
Barette in hair

GOLDIE
Blue and off-white striped cotton 20's style dress
w/white collar
Pin at neck
Cotton stockings
Off-white laced "sensible" shoes
Bib apron

BASIL
Steel rimmed glasses
Jacket length jean work jacket-very faded
Grey gabardine work trousers
Black belt
Blue and brown plaid flannel shirt
Ankle high black lace up boots
Old felt fedora
Handkerchief
White cotton socks

LUELLA
Pink hat w/flowers
Aqua-green cotton dress w/belt

Gray laced "sensible" shoes
Full rust apron
Handbag
Off-white sweater with embroidered flowers
Wedding ring
Cotton stockings

MELVIN
Overalls
Beige shirt
Work boots

DEWEY
Overalls
Blue work shirt
Work boots

*Important — All the clothes in *The Diviners* must look old and faded.

Also by Jim Leonard, Jr.

V and V Only

Anatomy of Gray

Crow and Weasel

Please consult samuelfrench.com for details

THE OFFICE PLAYS
Two full length plays by Adam Bock

THE RECEPTIONIST
Comedy / 2m., 2f. Interior

At the start of a typical day in the Northeast Office, Beverly deals effortlessly with ringing phones and her colleague's romantic troubles. But the appearance of a charming rep from the Central Office disrupts the friendly routine. And as the true nature of the company's business becomes apparent, The Receptionist raises disquieting, provocative questions about the consequences of complicity with evil.

"...Mr. Bock's poisoned Post-it note of a play."
- New York Times

"Bock's intense initial focus on the routine goes to the heart of *The Receptionist's* pointed, painfully timely allegory... elliptical, provocative play..."
- Time Out New York

THE THUGS
Comedy / 2m, 6f / Interior

The Obie Award winning dark comedy about work, thunder and the mysterious things that are happening on the 9th floor of a big law firm. When a group of temps try to discover the secrets that lurk in the hidden crevices of their workplace, they realize they would rather believe in gossip and rumors than face dangerous realities.

"Bock starts you off giggling, but leaves you with a chill."
- Time Out New York

"... a delightfully paranoid little nightmare that is both more chillingly realistic and pointedly absurd than anything John Grisham ever dreamed up."
- New York Times

NO SEX PLEASE, WE'RE BRITISH
Anthony Marriott and Alistair Foot

Farce / 7 m., 3 f. / Int.

A young bride who lives above a bank with her husband who is the assistant manager, innocently sends a mail order off for some Scandinavian glassware. What comes is Scandinavian pornography. The plot revolves around what is to be done with the veritable floods of pornography, photographs, books, films and eventually girls that threaten to engulf this happy couple. The matter is considerably complicated by the man's mother, his boss, a visiting bank inspector, a police superintendent and a muddled friend who does everything wrong in his reluctant efforts to set everything right, all of which works up to a hilarious ending of closed or slamming doors. This farce ran in London over eight years and also delighted Broadway audiences.

"Titillating and topical."
- "NBC TV"

"A really funny Broadway show."
- "ABC TV"

THE SCENE
Theresa Rebeck

Little Theatre / Drama / 2m, 2f / Interior Unit Set
A young social climber leads an actor into an extra-marital
affair, from which he then creates a full-on downward spiral
into alcoholism and bummery. His wife runs off with his best
friend, his girlfriend leaves, and he's left with… nothing.

"Ms. Rebeck's dark-hued morality tale contains enough fresh
insights into the cultural landscape to freshen what is essen-
tially a classic boy-meets-bad-girl story."
- New York Times

"Rebeck's wickedly scathing observations about the sort of
self-obsessed New Yorkers who pursue their own interests at
the cost of their morality and loyalty."
- New York Post

"The Scene is utterly delightful in its comedic performances,
and its slowly unraveling plot is thought-provoking and gut-
wrenching."
- Show Business Weekly

THREE MUSKETEERS
Ken Ludwig

All Groups / Adventure / 8m, 4f (doubling) / Unit sets
This adaptation is based on the timeless swashbuckler by Alexandre Dumas, a tale of heroism, treachery, close escapes and above all, honor. The story, set in 1625, begins with d'Artagnan who sets off for Paris in search of adventure. Along with d'Artagnan goes Sabine, his sister, the quintessential tomboy. Sent with d'Artagnan to attend a convent school in Paris, she poses as a young man – d'Artagnan's servant – and quickly becomes entangled in her brother's adventures. Soon after reaching Paris, d'Artagnan encounters the greatest heroes of the day, Athos, Porthos and Aramis, the famous musketeers; d'Artagnan joins forces with his heroes to defend the honor of the Queen of France. In so doing, he finds himself in opposition to the most dangerous man in Europe, Cardinal Richelieu. Even more deadly is the infamous Countess de Winter, known as Milady, who will stop at nothing to revenge herself on d'Artagnan – and Sabine – for their meddlesome behavior. Little does Milady know that the young girl she scorns, Sabine, will ultimately save the day.